THE COVERED BRIDGE MYSTERY

Book 3 of The Middlebury Mystery Series

THE COVERED BRIDGE MYSTERY

Holly Yoder DeHerrera

The Middlebury Mystery Series:
Book 3

BLACKSIDE PUBLISHING
COLORADO SPRINGS, CO

Connect with Holly:

Facebook: www.facebook.com/AuthorHollyYoderDeherrera/
Blog/Website: https://hollyyoderdeherrera.wordpress.com
Closed Facebook Book Club: Middlebury Mystery Series Book Club

URL: www.blacksidepublishing.com

Ordering Information: Amazon and Ingram

Cover and book design by: Scoti Domeij

Printed in the United States of America

The Covered Bridge Mystery/Holly DeHerrera

Library of Congress Control Number: 2019919667

978-1-68355-015-0; 1-68355-015-3 *The Covered Bridge Mystery* (Trade Paper)

First Edition

Printed in the United States of America

Dedication

To Richard, my friend from my college days, who just so happened to have Down Syndrome. He asked me every day to marry him, and to be sure to wear a dress, high heels, and earrings. Richard taught me about open-mouth smiles and unabridged, uninhibited love. You are special in every sense of the word. God never makes mistakes—you are living proof of that.

GLOSSARY

Aendi: Aunt

Daad: Dad

Dawdy haus (dah-dee) haus (house): A small home for elderly parents built onto or near the main house. When Dawdi retires and sells the farm and main house to an adult child, he and his wife move into the dawdy haus.

"Des gut.": "That's good."

Grossdaadi (or Dawdi): Grandfather

Grossmammi (or Mammi): Grandmother

Maam: Mom

Old Order Mennonite: Refers to Mennonite groups who dress plainly, live off their land, and rely on harvesting food from their gardens to eat during winter. Their Christian faith centers on their church and community and rejects modern technology and 'worldly' distractions.

Onkel: Uncle

Prayer kapp: The see-through, starched white head covering Old Order Mennonite women wear.

Sewing Bee or Quilting Bee: A friends-and-family get-together, most often during fall and winter months, in which the girls and women hand stitch quilts as wedding or baby gifts for family members or for charitable causes.

Table of Mysterious Contents

CHAPTER 1

Disappeared — into Thin Air

SADIE AND I WALK side-by-side on the crunchy, dirt path leading to the covered bridge between Mammi Yoder's house and Aendi's bed and breakfast. My cousin walks with bouncy steps, the gauzy strings of her prayer kapp dancing a jig above each shoulder to the beat of the nippy morning air. She smiles at me with her best full-face grin. I can't help but smile back, liking the way her sky-blue eyes sparkle on this dull-sky morning. Our clumpy footsteps echo against the wooden plank sides and tin roof of the covered bridge, forming a shelter around and above us.

I belt out a loud, "Hello-o-o-o-o."

Without hesitation, my echo answers back with a clear, "Hello-o-o-o-o."

Aendi Hannah asked us to pay a short visit to Grossmammi Yoder, Mammi for short, who's under the weather with a cold. Aendi sent along a jar of her homemade chicken noodle soup, a sure cure for any sickness or ailment, including broken legs.

Snow spreads like an all-white wedding quilt on the land beside the road. Green threads of early grass sprout through here and there, teasing us with springtime around the corner. Up ahead the bridge points, like an eye at the end of a long telescope, toward the fields in the distance and neat square farms lining up in order.

We pass a sorry cluster of glossy blackbirds that huddle to the side, complaining in their high-pitched chittering, most likely about the weather. I smile considering their conversation.

"Poppy?" My cousin's blond eyebrows bunch together, no doubt wondering what on earth I'm grinning about when neither of us have uttered a word for a solid minute.

"Hmm...?"

"Have you heard the stories they tell about this bridge?"

Our footsteps squeak against the bridge's ancient, timber boards as we enter its covering.

"Like what?" My cape dress, thin prayer kapp, and thick tights prove no match for the frigid air. I puff a little, watching my breath invade the cold, with a cloud of fog, then disappear.

"Like sounds and strange things left behind ... clothing ... and food."

"People toss trash all the time. What's so interesting about that?" I tug together the front of my black, hand-me-down sweater, knit by Maam for my older sister, now long-married with babies of her own.

"Well, it's just..."

"What?" I face my cousin, lifting an eyebrow. I perfected the fine art of lifting only one eyebrow, since I know it makes me appear intriguing and mysterious. I practiced long and hard in the small bathroom hand mirror I use to check that no stray hairs stick out on the top of my head.

"Things that were found often went missing someplace else."

"Oh?" I stop and wait for Sadie to explain.

"Like Mammi, for example. She said one of her tin buckets to feed the chickens disappeared into thin air. Guess where it turned up?"

Shadows and creepy-crawlies suddenly seem more creepy and crawly inside the dusky-dark covered passage of the bridge. "Here?" I squeak.

She nods, then glances behind her and tugs my arm to keep moving.

The tunnel of the covered bridge stretches into the distance, every sound magnified by one-thousand-one-hundred-eighty-two percent. A gust of wind whips against my face. The old wooden covering groans against the biting breeze. An ambitious crow takes flight, scattering the whole mess of them, and stirring up a frightful chorus of caw, caw, caws, triggering me to nearly leap out of my cape dress.

"I don't believe in nonsense. I'm too practical," I say too loud, then gulp–hard, as I steal a quick glance into the inky shadows behind me to make sure. I'm practical, but not a complete and total dummy. Sadie and I speed up, scurrying fast enough that you'd have to jog to keep up.

We step into the lamp-lit room. "Mammi," I call out.

Bundled in a navy-blue afghan, my Grossmammi's prayer kapp looks more like a rumpled piece of tissue paper than the neat, starched head covering usually donning her head. She leans toward us and smiles, her nose cherry-red. On the far wall a fire crackles in the wood stove, warming the whole space like the sun decided to visit.

"Well, if it isn't two of my favorite

mischief makers." She extends a shaky hand, gripping mine, her skin silky soft in my palm. I kneel in front of her, placing the jar of soup on the floor by her feet.

"We brought you Aendi's famous chicken noodle soup."

"Why, that's just what I need. Known to heal any ailment, you know. Even broken legs."

"Exactly." I tuck Mammi's blanket more tightly around her. "Want some?"

Mammi smiles, the wrinkles around her face embracing her grin. "Why, of course I do."

I plop on the floor in front of Mammi as Sadie settles on the shabby couch. "Where's Dawdi?" My cousin asks.

Mammi waves a hand. "Most likely puttering in the barn. He loves those horses you know." She chuckles. "He's bound and determined that they understand what he says and that they speak back."

"Really?" Sadie snatches a butter mint from Mammi's always-present glass bowl.

"Yes, sir-e-Bob."

My cousin pops up like a groundhog looking for spring and turns to head outside. "I'll go tell Dawdi we're here and we brought soup." Sadie has a soft spot for animals herself, so I'm not surprised she dashes to the barn. True to fashion, my cousin allows the front door to swing shut behind her, the door banging against the frame. "Sorry." I hear her shout from outside.

"Mammi, what's this I hear about your bucket going missing?"

She clears her throat, which still sounds scratchy. "It's more than that. Buckets, clothing from the wash line, even a pie I left cooling on the front patio. It's strange, that's for sure."

I rise from the floor and settle into the couch, the springs inside sounding like an out-of-tune guitar. "Could someone have taken it? Like Aendi Grace or Onkel Irvin?" Mammi and Dawdi Yoder live snug in the dawdy haus, a little apartment attached to my Aendi Grace and Onkel Irvin's home.

She shakes her head, her blood-shot, blue eyes wide. "No, we asked everyone. Nobody figured out how the items disappeared. And the most recent mystery, a quilt hanging on the line, went missing last week. Just before that, your Aendi and Onkel left to visit family in Ohio, so it wasn't them."

I swallow, my throat dry like it's filled with sand. "And where would you say they went? The things you lost." I don't want to hear the answer. Not really. But I have to know.

"Well, it's the strangest thing. Some of them were found at the covered bridge." At that Mammi breaks into a spasm of coughing, covering her mouth with a hankie stitched with little green clovers along the frilly edge.

"Here, Mammi." I lift the glass of water setting on her side table and place it in her hands.

She swigs small sips of the cold well water, and then hands the empty glass back to me, resting her head back on the chair.

"Have you been taking Elderberry Syrup?" Maam gives me that advice all the time at the slightest hint of sickness.

"Before every meal." She pats my hand. "Not to worry, Poppy. I won't kick the bucket just yet, I figure." She cackles, then gags, then spends a significant amount of time clearing her throat.

"I'll go warm the soup." I'm eager to press for more information, but I can't bear to be the reason for Mammi's hacking cough. She needs to rest, that's for sure.

"Thank you, dear." Before I can count to ten her stuffy-nosed-snore rattles the quiet of the little room.

Poor Mammi. I shuffle to the plain, brown laminate-floored kitchen, with my soup jar in hand. I twist the stove knob. The tick, tick, hiss of the gas ignites into a dancing-blue flame. I rummage through the cabinets and notice a pressure cooker, then shudder.

Maam's told me all about that dangerous tool whose top can explode, knocking out any old person happening by at the moment of doom, expelling spurts of steam explosions into the air like Mt. Vesuvius. Maam said her great Aendi nearly met her Maker that way, but ended up with only a few splatter-shaped burns and a shattered kitchen window.

I slam the cabinet door on the pressure cooker, so it knows how I feel about its existence, then keep hunting. I finally find a soup pot, then dump the contents of the Mason jar in the heavy-duty pot. I stir the healing concoction with a dark, dinged-up wooden spoon old enough to be my Mammi's great-great-Mammi.

While teeny-tiny bubbles form on the surface, I search for some bread to dunk in the soup. A loaf sits in the metal-lined bread drawer in the cabinet, like an offering from heaven, so golden and perfect.

As I cut the bread, I imagine a long beam of sunlight landing on it, like God himself placed it there. No doubt it was dropped off by one of our many extended family members who all live within buggy distance of one another.

With a serrated knife, I slice thick pieces, and slather them with lemony-yellow butter, then turn to check the soup. From the other room, I hear Mammi's snores sawing louder than Daad's less-than-healthy, gas-powered buzz saw.

Her words tumble around in my brain, like the tiny pebbles in the creek bottom near Sadie's house. *What kind of creep would steal from Mammi or Dawdi? And why leave all the evidence so near, just inside the covered bridge, for anyone to find—almost like the person wants it to be spotted?*

I stare into the pot, the bubbles billowing and churning the thick soup, and I'm reminded of volcanoes again, and second degree burns. I reach to grab a bowl, ladling in the hot mixture. Then I shuffle into the living room with the bread and soup resting on a bamboo tray.

Sure, the warm soup heals sickness, but it does nothing to calm my jumbled thoughts. First off, who's stealing from innocent people and, second, when will he or she strike next? ✳

CHAPTER 2

WHAT'S THAT NOISE?

A HOWLING BLAST WHIPS about outside while Mammi, Dawdi, Sadie, and I sit around the living room. The blowing snow cascades in sheets so thick the barn is no longer visible through the large, side picture window. I look at Dawdi, who stares at the unexpected blizzard.

"Well, girls, I don't imagine you'll be heading home anytime soon." Against the low rumble of the wind a humming sound fills the small living room.

"What's that?" Sadie asks.

Dawdi looks down as if trying to locate the source of the noise. "Oh, this thing." He pulls a small, cellular phone from his front pocket and fumbles with the buttons before saying a way-too-loud, "Hello?"

I cover my mouth not wanting Dawdi to notice I'm laughing. He looks super silly with the modern technology pressed against his bearded face. Since as long as I can remember, his plain black wool hat with a notch nicked on one side of the brim covered his shaggy, white hair. He bellows on the cell phone loud enough to be heard clear on the other side of the farm.

I listen to his responses. "All right then. I imagine this thing'll be dead before tomorrow. The battery's flashin' already." He moves his head up and down, like the person on the other end of the line can see him nodding "yes." Then he grunts and nods again.

What does Dawdi know about cell phones? Plain folk like ourselves don't own them, at least not most of us. Sadie's family does, because of their bed and breakfast business, but that's unusual.

Most of us don't even have electricity, just gas-powered stoves and lights.

Dawdi fusses with the phone for a solid minute before nodding and turning his attention to us. "That was your maam, Poppy. She gave me this doohickey while Aendi Grace and Onkel Irvin are in Ohio. Didn't want us 'not to have communication' in case of a problem, I suppose. It's a whole lot of nonsense. I'm glad to have it, though, so they know you're all right and not to come out in this weather to rescue you."

Sadie fidgets and shoots me a curious look.

"Your maam said she wants you two to stay put for the night. Hopefully things will clear up by tomorrow." Dawdi shoves the phone back into the pocket on his loose-fitting shirt.

All of a sudden, excitement rushes into my chest. It will be like the old days when Sadie and I had sleepovers at their house. I elbow Sadie and whisper, "Maybe we can go play with some of Mammi's stuff in the basement."

Sadie smiles, raising her eyebrows. "Her dress up things?"

"Yah." I don't know how happy our parents are about Mammi's private stash of fancy hats and shiny purses, with us being plain and Old Order Mennonites and all. Maybe they decided there's no harm in making believe, or else they knew Mammi wouldn't back down from having a little corner of fun for the grandkids.

"Do you need anything, Mammi?" I ask.

"No, I'm going to rest my eyes. No fun for you two hanging around us old fogies. Might as well find something else to do." She laughs, but her coughing stops that right quick.

"Well, if you're sure."

Dawdi pipes up, "And when you're done, I'm going to make my famous hot cocoa with big fat marshmallows. Maybe we'll even talk your Mammi into joining us for a game of Pig Mania." Dawdi's squinty-eyed smile makes me happy. He relaxes in his recliner with his button-up shirt all neat and tucked and his black suspenders drawn tight over his slightly hunched shoulders.

Sadie hops up and down. "That sounds really fun, Dawdi."

With another grunt and a wink, he reaches for the *Farmer's Almanac* on his side table. Before we shoot out the door, he begins his aimless whistling while Mammi's soft snoring weaves in and out of Dawdi's tune "Old MacDonald." ✳

CHAPTER 3

WHO WANTS TO HURT MAMMI AND DAWDI?

"I LOVE THIS PURSE." I lift up a super old, glossy black handbag, then snap open the tarnished silver clasp, and peek inside. Grocery lists, notepads, and carbon copies of receipts written in childish handwriting fill the bag. "Oh, these are from when we were really little and played store."

Sadie giggles as she positions a small, round hat with a mesh veil and black feather on her head. "How do I look?" She says in her best posh-lady accent.

"You look divine, darling."

Sadie covers her mouth as she snickers. "Where'd you hear that?"

"You know, that diner in town? The one with the yummy pie, where they play old black and white movies all the time?"

"Oh, yes, The Pantry. I love their blueberry pie."

"Well, I heard it on the TV they have hanging on the wall. They sure said 'daaaah-ling' a lot in those days."

"Well, dah-ling, what shall we play?"

"Want to pretend to be detectives? We can write our clues on these notepads."

Sadie reaches for a little flip top, paper tablet. "Sure. We can begin solving the covered bridge mystery."

"Oooh, yah. Mammi told me a little more."

"Really? Tell me. Tell me."

I fill Sadie in on the other missing items. "I wish we had more clues to go on besides a few stolen things. Well, let's list everything that's missing and the possible suspects."

"Suspects?" My cousin asks.

"You know, who could have done it."

Sadie scratches something on the paper. "Suspect #1, Caleb." She smiles and blushes.

"From our school?"

"Well, you never know." Sadie smirks.

"Well, I guess, but why would Caleb do that? He's really nice." Now it's my turn to blush. "And he has what he needs. And he lives waaaay down the road."

Sadie sighs. "Fine, I'll scratch him off. Do we know anyone who's poor?"

"Well, little Joseph from the grade below ours lost his Daad last year. I heard they might move to be closer to family who can help them. I noticed a hole in his collar last week."

Sadie jots down, "Joseph," then looks at me. "Anyone else?"

The heaviness of guilt blankets my chest from accusing Joseph and I swallow an unexpected lump. He's super small for his age because of some disease and he keeps to himself mostly. Deep down, I know he'd never do such a thing.

My mind wanders from Joseph to the neighbors living closest to Mammi and

Dawdi Yoder. "What about the Schmidt's, just down the road?"

Sadie shakes her head, "All their kids are grown and gone. Do you think a grown adult would go around swiping pies?"

"You never know, Sadie, desperate people do desperate stuff."

"Okay, I'll write their names down, but I don't think they're the ones," she says shaking her head.

Usually I'm the reasonable one. I eye my too-wise cousin, then lean in to look at her list. "How about I start a list of all the reasons a person would take those things. So, clothing, a quilt, a bucket, and a pie."

"Because they want to sell them?" Sadie offers.

"Good thinking, cousin. What else?"

"They need them for themselves?"

"Yah, or . . ." A twisty feeling knots in my stomach. "Or because they want to hurt Mammi and Dawdi for some reason. Or Aendi Grace and Onkel Irvin."

Sadie's eyes grow wide, a little scared like our dog Maxwell when the tiny cousins chase him around the yard. "Why would anyone want to hurt them?"

"No clue. They're probably the nicest people in the whole wide world."

"Yah, that's the truth."

"Well . . ." Sadie stares at the small basement window with snow piled halfway up the glass.

"With all that snow, if we get stuck here for the weekend, we might find tracks if anyone's snooping around."

Sadie looks back at me. "You mean, out there? Tonight? You think someone will sneak around in the blizzard tonight?" Her voice takes on a near-squeak.

"No, not tonight. Too gusty. But maybe early in the morning, once the worst of the storm passes."

The wind moans low, then high through the small window, raising goose bumps on our arms like Mammi's beaded purse. Sadie springs up quick as a jack-in-the-box.

I link my arm through Sadie's, keeping an eye on the window and whisper, "Tomorrow morning, first thing, let's check for tracks. After we make breakfast for Mammi and Dawdi, that is. Let's look for any footprints in the snow. It's our job to help Mammi and Dawdi right now. Especially if someone means them any harm."

If we find any tracks, they might lead us straight to the criminal's hide-out though. And then where would we be? In deep, dark danger, that's what. ✳

CHAPTER 4

WHO'S SLINKING AROUND IN THE DARK?

THE SKY IS A grey smudge before the sun rises above the trees to shine over the farm. A crunching sound rattles me from my sleep. The thin windows of the downstairs guest room did nothing last night to shut out the sound of the wailing wind and does nothing this morning to muffle the noise of what sounds like feet crunching on brittle snow.

I manage to pull myself to the windowsill above the guest bed Sadie and I shared last night. I attempt to catch a glimpse of whatever made the noise. I'm freezing in the thin nighty Dawdi dug up for me from Mammi's sleepover stash. Dark shadows slant across the flat space between the house and the barn. The normally cheerful yard appears scary and strange. My eyes adjust to the blackness. Finally, I make out what looks like a slumped figure, slogging his way to the barn. My heart flutters like a crow trying to break out of a too-small cage.

"Sadie," I hiss, wanting a witness to make sure I'm not imagining things.

"The purse is too shiny," she mumbles into her pillow.

Sadie isn't the quickest to wake from her sleep. I nudge her with my foot, not wanting to leave the window. "Sadie, get up."

She sits up like a rag doll, all fabric and no bones. "What, Poppy?"

"There's someone outside."

Sadie springs out of bed with surprising speed and joins me at the sill. "Where?"

"There." I point.

The hunched figure ducks into the barn, leaving the door open like a mouth catching flies.

I turn to my cousin. "What on earth do we do?"

"Let's get Dawdi."

"Okay." I nod, even though Sadie's not looking at me. She still stares out the window like she's drilling a hole through the glass with her eyeballs.

Then a terrible thought strikes me. "What if this person means to hurt Dawdi? I don't want to send him into the darkness with no way to protect himself."

"You're right." Sadie turns to look at me, her long hair fanning across her shoulders like a veil. "So what do we do?"

I squeeze her hand. "We pray and pray, then tell Dawdi tomorrow morning." I swallow against my fear. "And let's watch until we know that person's gone, okay?"

Sadie only nods. *Is she about to cry?*

"Not to worry, cousin. God is watching over us, for sure." I whisper with as much confidence as I can muster.

But my words don't stop the twisting, squeezing tangle in my tummy or the shudder. My chest whirls like a hamster on a wheel—running and running like its life depends on it. ✳

CHAPTER 5

THE THIEF STRIKES — AGAIN

SADIE AND I KNEEL on our beds looking out the window until we both doze off, knees locked and our droopy heads propped on our folded arms. By the time we both awake, the sun shines bright enough that I know we slept through breakfast.

We shuffle into the living room to find Mammi in the same chair, but dressed in clean clothes and looking a little more chipper with a pressed prayer kapp on her head. Her hands cradle a cup of mint tea.

"Sorry, Mammi. We overslept." I lean over to plant a kiss on her head.

"Not to worry, girls. That was a frightful storm last night. It would take a deaf person to have slept through it. Which is probably why I snoozed like a baby without a problem." She sucks a loud sip of her tea and grins.

"Mammi, you're not deaf," Sadie says.

"Oh, maybe you're right, but somehow I managed to get some shut-eye."

"Have you eaten breakfast?" I look toward the kitchen.

"Yes. Your Dawdi made his corn fritters with maple syrup for me. There's a pile for you two."

My mouth waters like Niagara Falls during the rainy season. "Oh goodness, I love Dawdi's fritters. I'm sure sorry we weren't up to help."

"Oh, your Dawdi enjoys cooking. He's funny, that man. But I'm glad for it. Especially when I prefer to stay planted like a sack of flour on this chair for now."

Sadie and I devour the fritters, then dress and head into the white, glittery morning in search of Dawdi. Along the way we scan for footprints and spot Dawdi's large, feet tracks trailing from the back door to the barn. Then we notice another set of footsteps coming from the road. Sparkling snow still falls, but slower, as if last night wore the blizzard out and it's ready for bed.

"Look, Sadie." I kneel to get a better look. "They're a bit bigger than my feet."

"How big is that?" Sadie grins at me. I know she's teasing me, because it's common knowledge that I have the biggest clunkers of all the girls in the family.

I smack her arm. "I wear a size 10 ladies, so maybe these are size 12?"

Sadie giggles and says, "Not too big if a boy snooped around last night."

"Very funny. I can't tell anything else about the shoes. The snow filled in the pattern on the sole."

"Hmm."

"Well, stinky, I guess the shoe print is a clue, but not a great one," I say, deflated.

"Let's follow the trail they made." Sadie points to telltale footsteps in the glittery snow.

"Good thinking." We follow the fresh

imprints to the road when a neighbor glides by on a horse-drawn sleigh, smudging any tracks clean away.

"Yah, we've narrowed the suspect down to around a hundred people on this road alone."

"Well, that combined with other clues we find might lead us to something," I offer, hoping to sound optimistic.

"Or someone . . ." Sadie shivers and tugs me toward the barn. "Come on, let's talk to Dawdi."

"I don't know, cousin."

Sadie steps into the entry, paying no attention to my hesitation. I watch the back of her prayer kapp dusted with a thin powder of snow. After the bright-white, morning sunshine, I blink against the darkness and the dust-bunny-dingy inside the barn.

Dawdi's suspender-crisscrossed back hunches over his tools. The back of his black hat, notch-free, casts a shadow on his neck. The side of his face appears in great concentration. He doesn't even turn when the wind kicks the barn door shut like a trap. I walk to him so we're side-by-side and lay my hand on his gnarled, work-worn knuckles. He flinches and notices we're in the barn, blinking like he's knocked out of a trance.

"Dawdi?"

"Poppy." He looks at me dazed, his eyelids fluttering several times.

"You okay?"

He scrunches his eyebrows. "Well, I don't know."

"What is it?" Sadie asks from the other side of Dawdi.

"I could have promised I put all my tools away. I always keep them just so, smallest wrenches to largest ones. Small screwdrivers to big. Look here." He points a thick finger, rimmed with grease from all his tinkering on farm equipment. "See anything missing?" The black space in the middle of the tools makes it so obvious that something's not there.

"A wrench is gone missing?" I ask.

"Yes, Poppy, and my Grossdawdi

Yoder gave me that wrench. And even more strange? My old beat up hat disappeared too. Who'd want that old thing?" Creases pile-up on his forehead from his bunched-up expression.

"Weren't you wearing that hat last night?"

Dawdi scratches the side of his forehead. "I did a last check on the horses before bedtime and set it on my workbench. I musta grabbed this spare hat by accident. I keep it hanging on a hook just in case."

I'm not sure what "in case" he means, but nod anyway.

Sadie bounces on her toes. "You don't think . . . ?"

I frown, not happy about this one bit. I shake my head to squelch her thought, to beg her not to say it out loud. Dawdi appears plenty rattled already.

"You don't think it's the same thing that's happened, Dawdi, with all the other missing things? You don't think it's the thief, do you?"

So much for my cousin taking a hint.

Dawdi grunts, clears his throat and says half grunt, half words, "Well, I don't know about that."

I shake my head again at Sadie, but she ignores me and adds, "What is this, the fifth thing that's gone missing?"

"Don't know. Haven't kept track. But something strange sure is going on around here."

Sadie, intent on finishing her thoughts, puts in, "Yah, and did you see the big footprints out front?"

Dawdi closes his eyes like thinking about the big footprints might just cause him to stumble. "No. No, I didn't," he says, sounding tired.

I reach behind Dawdi to pinch the back of Sadie's arm.

"Ow. What on earth, Poppy?"

"Let's let Dawdi finish what he's doing." I pierce her with my best be-quiet-or-I'll-really-pinch-you look.

Sadie opens her mouth, then shuts it like she's a fish instead of a girl. Then she nods, turns around, and stomps away. She's so mad at me, I imagine steam blowing out her nose and ears.

Out in the cold air she whirls around and yells, "What's wrong with talking to Dawdi?" Her cheeks blaze red. "It's his stuff, Poppy. He knows about stuff going missing already."

I reach for Sadie's hand. "We don't need to freak out Dawdi and Mammi. What good would that do?" Her hand wilts like a limp rag in mine.

"You hurt me, Poppy." She jerks her hand back and rubs at her arm.

I pull her into a hug. "I'm sorry, cousin. I didn't mean to, honest. I only wanted to tell you to stop talking about it. Didn't you see the scared look on Dawdi's face?"

Sadie resists, then steps back. "No."

"I'm sorry. Is your arm okay?"

"Yes," she mumbles.

"Can you forgive me for being a big pooper-scooper?"

This brings a tiny smile. "You were a pooper-scooper."

I offer, "Friends again?"

She grins. "Fine. Next time, don't pinch me."

"Alright."

Sadie and I trudge around in the snow enjoying the crisp, freezing air tingling inside our noses. I say, "Why, Sadie? Why keep stealing a whole bunch of random stuff with nothing in common?"

"I don't know," she blurts in a near-wail. "Makes me really mad."

"Yah, me too. Dawdi and Mammi don't deserve this."

Sadie stops and turns to me, looking like a bull facing a crimson-red cape. "We have to find out who's doing this to Dawdi and Mammi and stop them, okay?"

"I agree." But even as I say it, something tumbles in my gut. *Will stopping someone so cold-hearted mean danger for all of us?* ✳

CHAPTER 6

WHO WILL PROTECT MAMMI AND DAWDI?

WE SPEND THE MORNING tidying Mammi's kitchen, prepping a pot of stew for lunch, and organizing her pantry. Sadie lifts a jar of her Maam's famous peach butter and grins. "I love to eat this on fresh bread."

"Want to make some so we can snack on it later? Well, Dawdi and Mammi too, of course. I have an easy recipe that doesn't take all day to make."

After mixing together all the ingredients and kneading the dough, we set the lump aside to rise in bread pans and cover them with a see-through layer of plastic wrap to keep in the warmth and to encourage a good puffy rise.

"Let's walk around outside. I'm ready for some fresh air."

We step into the sunshiny afternoon and spot cousin Jonah hauling logs of wood to a splitting stump. He swings his ax, slicing the halves like they were sticks of butter instead of big ole chunks of tree.

"Hi, Poppy, Sadie." Jonah waves his large hand at us and beams. "What'cha doing here?"

"We came to bring Mammi some soup and ended up staying the night on account of the storm," Sadie offers.

"Oh, yah, that was a doozy, for sure. And with it already April and all. Old man winter musta wanted a little more attention." At that Jonah snorts, then slaps his leg, as is his special way. At nearly eighteen, Jonah is tall and strong and does the chores of a man. But as Maam once told me, "He has the special gift of still thinking like a child."

Always will, I suppose. I like Jonah's kind face and ready smile. *Child or not, he's one of my most favorite people in the entire world.*

Jonah wipes his forehead with the back of his sleeve, leaving a smear of dirt streaked across his brow. He picks up another log and buries the ax in the end of the wood, splitting it down the middle with another powerful *whoosh.* I figure he's here to help, like us, taking care of the heavy jobs while Onkel Irvin is away.

"Wanna join us for some bread and Aendi Hannah's famous peach butter later on?"

Jonah stares toward the covered bridge and rubs his neck, leaving a smudge of dirt there too. "Sure. That's fine, Poppy." Then Jonah's face collapses, swallowing his smile. "Did'ja know Mammi and Dawdi refuse to lock their barn, not even their house, at night? Think you might talk to them 'bout that?" Lines edge his round, brown eyes. "It's not right, them being so careless."

I kick at the snow sagging all around in

heaps, like it lost all its strength against the afternoon sunshine. "What's got you concerned, Jonah?" Does he know about the thefts? I don't want to stir him up more than he already is.

"Aw . . . just wish they'd listen, but when I bring it up they say the Lord is their per-tection. How's come they don't care about any ol' person harming them?"

I shake my head, knowing that's their thinking, even though I don't really understand it either.

"What if someone does something the good Lord doesn't want? Like breaking in and getting to them? Daad says God gives us a choice." Jonah holds his calloused hands palms out, his round eyes wide, ticking off the two choices on his two pointer fingers. "Pick God and live fer Him. Or pick selfish ways and do whatever you want. So that means someone can choose to hurt Mammi and Dawdi." He drops his arms, snags another log, placing the fat end on the chopping block. Jonah then swoops the long-handled ax into the heart of the wood and two pieces fly apart, driving his point home.

Shivers dance up my arms. I wrap my sweater in tighter. Maybe Jonah can help us solve the mystery. "Have you heard, then?"

"'Bout what?" Jonah tosses the split log pieces into the growing pile.

"About the stuff that's gone missing?" Sadie whisper-yells.

Jonah rubs his forehead more vigorously. "I've heard." He eyeballs me like I have the answer to this pickle. "Only makes my point. Can't you get them to listen, Poppy? You're good at that sort of thing." He says it like I can make a grown adult stop doing what they've done since the beginning of, well, forever.

"I'll try, Jonah. In the meantime, how about you keep a look out and let us know if you see anything suspicious." Jonah nods in agreement, then focuses on the rhythm of splitting the pile of logs in front of him—stand, inhale, swing, chop, toss, stand, inhale, swing, chop, toss.

Sadie and I leave Jonah to his work. My insides feel all scrambled. "Jonah seems pretty worked up. I wonder if he knows something more than he's saying."

"I was thinking the same thing," Sadie says.

What could be so bad that my cousin can't bring himself to spit it out? ✳

CHAPTER 7

MAMMI AND DAWDI IGNORE THE DANGER

DAWDI, MAMMI, POPPY, JONAH, and I sit around the living room coffee table munching the fresh-baked bread slathered with peach jam and not doing much talking. I eye the plain, wood-paneled walls, wondering about the thief. *Why would anyone steal things from someone who doesn't have many worldly possessions?* Dawdi and Mammi aren't poor, but they don't collect junk—only the things they need.

Sadie says around a mouthful of food, interrupting my thoughts, "Should we head home this afternoon, Mammi? Or will you be needing our help some more?"

Mammi, perched like a small owl in an enormous nest, leans her head back against the easy chair. Her hair wisps around her face like itty-bitty feathers. She says with a scratch in her voice, "I'm okay, girls. I do love you being around. How 'bout you decide?" She finishes her bite, washing it down with a swig of hot mint tea.

Sadie looks at me and I look at Jonah. He clears his throat and announces in his typical, too-loud voice, "They need you here for sure, Poppy." Dawdi smiles knowingly, like Jonah's over-protective nature tickles him instead of annoys him. "For sure," Jonah adds like he wants to make sure we get the point.

"Did you tell Jonah about the missing tool, Dawdi?" Sadie asks.

My Dawdi squirms in his seat like a briar poked him in the backside, then settles into the chair. "No need to worry Jonah. Nor your mammi." He grunts like the matter is settled.

"What's this, Isaac?" Mammi's eyebrows lift for a split second.

Dawdi pats her hand like she is five instead of eighty-two. "Nothing to worry over, dear."

Jonah bounces in his seat. "Yes, it is something to worry over." He practically hollers the words, then stops abruptly and covers his flushed face. "Sorry, Dawdi."

We all sit still. The clock ticks as loud as a summer grasshopper rubbing its wings together.

Mammi looks around the room, "What aren't you all telling me?"

Dawdi speaks up, "Only that something else is missing. Nothing to worry over."

"Tomorrow has enough worries of its own," Mammi says as if that's all there is to it, then stands as slow as an unfolding leaf. "And some poor soul out there seems bent on getting every last thing he can from us. But I say, if he needs it, he's welcome to it."

Dawdi nods and stands beside his wife. "Wise words."

Together they link arms and mosey to the kitchen as if both know what the other needs. More tea or bread. Or maybe just company.

Jonah shoots up like a giant tree. "See what I mean? They don't listen." With that he stomps back into the snowy afternoon leaving a half-eaten slice of bread behind. Very un-Jonah like. ✳

CHAPTER 8

Running Scared

"DON'T YOU THINK WE should turn back?" Sadie tugs her sleeves over her fingers and tucks her hands under her armpits.

"I want to see if maybe some of the missing things are inside the covered bridge, like people say." I want to see, but I *don't* want to see. A screech owl shrieks a spooky, shrill hoot, then flutters into the sky near the dark, open mouth of the covered bridge. I search the dusky evening horizon to make sure we're alone.

Something rustles below the covered bridge, where the ground drops toward the swift-running creek.

Sadie grabs my arm, snagging me back. "What . . . what was that?"

"Don't know." I clear my throat around the frog stuck there.

"Maybe we should go back to Mammi and Dawdi's."

I gulp down the frog and squeak, "It's nothing, I'm sure. Besides, we've come this far."

A hint of sap and damp bark penetrates the nippy night air and envelops me in a foggy blanket of darkness, all tangly brush and, I pray, no criminals lurking in the gloom. Only I'm not so sure, so I talk loud and confident to scare off whatever or whoever might hover near the base of the bridge. Maybe a raccoon rambling about on a jaunt. "Sure is a nice night for a stroll," I nearly bellow.

"Shhh," Sadie hisses.

"We can't show fear. They'll smell it," I caution.

"Who will smell it?" Sadie whisper-wails.

"You know, any wild animals."

"Poppy, what sort of wild animals live around here in Middlebury?"

I sense the hysterics Sadie might cave into should I voice my theory: A cougar or a crazed thief who might not appreciate being cornered by two girls. The crook might decide to attack us rather than give up his hiding place with all his loot.

"Oh, you know, squirrels. Or raccoons."

Sadie huffs into the half-way-between-day-and-night air. "Poppy, there's nothing scary about a squirrel." She sounds partly relieved, partly annoyed. "Why do you have to do that?"

"Do what?" I spin on my sneaker and look at my cousin's gray-peach face in the waning light. The shadows cast by the moon make the spaces below her eyes, brows, and nose look almost like tiny caves.

"Freak me out for no good reason, that's what."

I rub her arm and fake a laugh, sounding more like gagging on hot cocoa than anything resembling funny. "Sorry. My imagination can get the better of me."

"Yah, it can."

We inch forward using itty-bitty steps, like neither of us really want to go the direction we're headed. A dark pile slumps against a timber beam inside the opening of the bridge.

I flick on my flashlight and Sadie gasps. "Might have turned that on sooner."

"I kinda forgot about it." I sweep the torchlight across the blob covered in a quilt.

"Is that . . . ?"

"Yes. Yes, it is." Sadie's voice sounds low and miserable.

"Mammi's missing quilt."

"What's under it?" My cousin asks.

"Don't know." I imagine all sorts of horrible things. Cougars. Crazed criminals. A psycho squirrel colony willing to fight any passer-by for possession of the quilt.

"You go check." Sadie nudges my back.

"No, you go." I sound like I only want her to go because it's her turn, not because I fear I might pee if I lift the edge of the log-cabin-patterned blanket. Sadie refuses to budge.

I reach a trembling hand toward the blanket-enveloped blob and lift the soft, damp corner of Mammi's patchwork comforter. An enormous bang from below the bridge startles us. Sadie and I scream like two year olds, spin, and sprint full tilt to Mammi and Dawdi's. All the way. Without stopping.

Fear compels me to grip the blanket for dear life, like it can save me, the end dragging across the muddy, still snowy ground. By the time we reach the house, we both break into hysterical, freaked-out belly laughs, releasing our terror.

"What on earth was that?" Sadie gasps and stomps into the front entry. Steam still lingers around her mouth from the cold.

I shake my head. "No idea, but at least we got this." I wave the bedraggled-looking blanket under Sadie's nose. "Mammi will be so pleased."

"Yah, good thing you grabbed it. Did you

see what was under the quilt?" Sadie asks.

"No, didn't get a chance."

Sadie's voice drops to a curious whisper. "I wonder what was under it?"

"I wonder what made that terrible loud noise." My heart beats like a base drum in the Middlebury marching band. "Good thing we got home safe, Cousin."

"Yah. Good thing." ✳

CHAPTER 9

DARK AND STRANGE

WE LAY THE FILTHY, sorry-looking quilt in front of Mammi and Dawdi who sip tea in the living room unaware of our disturbing, mystery adventure. Dawdi leans forward on his cane rocker. "Now where did you find that?"

"At the covered bridge. Whoever took it must of stashed it there," I remark. *That means the thief stays nearby.* A chill ripples down my neck. I rub my hands up and down my sweatered arms and wait for Dawdi's thoughts.

"Probably some poor homeless soul, Isaac," Mammi warbles.

"I don't think so," Sadie says. "Why would he keep stealing random things? Like Dawdi's hat or the wrench?"

Dawdi shakes his head, then rubs his wrinkled, strong hand over his long, fluffy beard. "Still, we are called to show love to everyone. Not only the ones who make us happy." He touches Mammi's arm and says a little louder, "What do you think of washing this quilt and taking it back to the place where the girls found it. Maybe add in a few things too, like fresh bread or cookies. I'll even do the dropping off."

My mouth hangs open like a hinge on a trunk. "Say what?"

"Yah, say what?" Sadie squeaks.

Dawdi offers a kind smile and the wisdom lines around his eyes bunch together. "God's ways don't make a lot of sense sometimes, do they girls?"

Like two confused twins, we both shake our heads.

"What if this person needs more than our earthly belongings? What if he or she needs some love, just maybe?"

I can't help myself. I jump up and go to hug him, the sweetest Dawdi in the world. "You're so smart." For some reason my throat feels tight and full, like an enormous bread roll lodges in there.

"Well, I think you're all smart," Mammi adds.

We giggle in the quiet buzz of the gas lanterns hanging steadfast around the walls of the small room. Maybe, just maybe, a reminder to reflect light even when things seem dark and strange. ✳

CHAPTER 10

CAUGHT. RED-HANDED

SADIE AND I DECIDE to go home with the promise to return after school on Monday to bake a batch of my best cookie recipe, ginger molasses. Mammi's cold no longer reddens her nose like a raspberry and her eyes appear brighter, so we figure she's on the mend.

"Meet you at school tomorrow?" I say to Sadie, not wanting to leave my cousin, but needing to head home.

"Meet you at school tomorrow." She nods offering a parting hug.

The next day Sadie and I meet in the front foyer of our white, clapboard school housing kids, kindergarten to eighth grade. "What do you think of Dawdi's plan?"

Sadie tips her head to the side. "I like it. It's just like Dawdi." Her eyes look gray blue this morning and super-duper sparkly.

"Me too," I say, squeezing her hand before proceeding toward the cast-iron hooks along the length of the sidewall for kids to hang their coats and bonnets on. I unbutton my black cape coat and drape it on the hook, then untie my black, warm-weather bonnet, resting it on top. Somehow everyone knows where their bonnets and coats dangle, even though they all look the same.

Being plain means not standing out to gain unnecessary attention by being different. So, the same cloaks and bonnets for the girls line one half of the wall and the same coats and hats for the boys line the other half.

I look at the line of hanging winter attire. That's when I spot it—a larger hat with a telltale nick on one side, about an inch deep. *What is Dawdi's missing hat doing in the school house? Is the thief one of our very own friends?*

During lunch hour I fill Sadie in on the close threat of a criminal amongst our group. Is it a big eighth grader playing pranks? Maybe, but why keep going with it? No, stealing over and over again tells me we're dealing with a cold-hearted person, one who doesn't care one tiny bit for the feelings of innocent mammis and dawdis.

"Let's watch to see who grabs the hat after lunch. They're bound to want to head outside to play before the break is over," I whisper into Sadie's ear. She rubs the spot with her hand and giggles.

"Okay. We'll keep a look out. Only I'm really hungry. Can I eat first?"

"You eat while I keep watch, then we'll switch, 'kay?"

"'Kay." Sadie grabs her pail and heads into the classroom to scarf her smoked-turkey sandwich. Minutes later she returns with a yellow smear on her cheek.

"You have mustard on your face."

"Oh." She rubs at it frantically then asks, "Better?"

"Yes."

"I see the hat's still there," Sadie says, nodding her head in the direction of the coat hooks.

"Yah," I say. "I've been watching like a hawk. Maybe the thief saw me and got scared he'd get caught red-handed."

"Well, how about you go eat now and I'll stand outside and keep an eye out for someone coming out wearing the hat."

"Okay. I'll meet you on the playground in a few minutes." I inhale my ham salad sandwich, then head toward the door, checking the hooks before leaving.

The hat is gone.

I step outside, blinking against the light, momentarily blinded by the noontime sunshine. Then I spot Sadie, her cheeks flushed red from skipping rope with Rachel Bontrager.

When I reach my cousin, I holler, "Well, did you spot anything?"

"Anything, what?" Rachel asks in between a jump. She always likes nosing in everyone's business.

"Oh, nothing," I mumble.

Sadie doesn't say anything, only shakes her head back and forth.

"Have you been paying attention?"

"I have, Poppy, but I haven't seen anything."

"When I came out, Dawdi's hat wasn't on the hook, cousin."

At that Sadie slumps a little, her jump rope hangs limp in her hands, "Sorry."

I scan the half grassy, half-snowy schoolyard. My eye catches on Jessie, the biggest boy in the school. "There." I point.

The hat tops his bushy bowl hair cut. He laughs, then yanks it off his head. Jessie thrusts Dawdi's old hat into Caleb's hand, who plops it on his noggin, like he owns it, then walks away chuckling without handing it back.

"Noooooo. Not Caleb," Sadie whines.

"Yes, I'm afraid so, Sadie. We can't let his good looks make us miss what's right in front of us. Caleb is the thief. Besides that, he's plain out mean. He fooled both of us."

My ham salad sandwich churns in my stomach. Disappointment wallops me, like a slap in the face, a punch in the stomach, and a kick in the rear all at the same time.

"So much for Dawdi's sweet plan," I say. "He's known Caleb since he was born."

"Dawdi's gonna be heart broken." Sadie looks ready to cry.

"Should we tell him?" I can't stand to ruin my Dawdi's view of the world.

"Maybe not. I don't like him being disappointed. He's the nicest person in Middlebury."

I can't help but smile. "You're right, Sadie, he is. Let's wait and figure out this mystery for ourselves. We need to find a way to sneak to Caleb's house to see what else he might be stashing there. He lives quite a ways away from the covered bridge, but it's on the same road."

Caleb and some other boys huddle together now, talking, probably about all his new loot.

"Good point." Sadie scratches at a spot under her prayer kapp.

"That must be where he keeps everything, so nobody suspects he's the crook."

"Yah, true. Maybe we can bake an extra batch of cookies as an excuse to drop by his house. Maybe we'll find more stuff to make sure he's the one," I say.

"Of course, he's the one, Poppy. He's wearing the evidence." Sadie points in his direction just as Caleb looks our way.

I bat her hand down, then wave at Caleb like a weirdo. "True . . . let's see if we can find one more thing to prove he's guilty. Otherwise, he might deny the whole thing and say he bought the hat or something."

"It is a common hat, Poppy."

"Yes, but not the cut in the side, like Dawdi's was when it went missing." I realize I'm twisting the front of my sweater into a knot and drop my hands to my side. Sadie and I turn to walk into the schoolhouse.

"You're right. I wish you weren't right. You know?"

Rachel tags along, looking back and forth between us as we speak to find out what we're talking about.

"Yes, Sadie, I know all too well," I say through a grown-up sounding sigh.

Rachel scratches her head, then gives up, and stomps her feet on the steps to remove some of the slushy mud.

My cousin and I link arms and step inside. Caleb stands there with a few of the other boys, laughing like he isn't a big, fat jerk. I offer my worst glare, which he ignores.

Criminals don't care about glares, I discover, or about much else, including wiping their feet on the mat before tracking mud through the entire school. They're just selfish that way. ✳

CHAPTER 11

KiLL Them WiTh KiNDNEss

OUR HEARTS AREN'T INTO the baking. What starts as Dawdi's super-sweet idea turns into a really sour-as-lemons project. Who wants to bake ginger molasses cookies for someone who purposely stole from someone you love, then waltzes around bragging to all the boys about it?

The hand-wound timer rings with a loud ding, jangling my nerves, which are as skittery as a crawdad on the edge of the creek bank.

"Would it have been so bad to add two cups of salt instead of sugar?" Sadie mutters.

"Yes. It would be bad," I say. Then I can't

stifle the giggle that escapes. "But fun."

My cousin loosens the cookies with a thin, metal spatula then gently moves each one to a cooling rack.

"Besides . . ." I take a bite of my favorite recipe to test to make sure they're good enough to give away. "We're taking a batch to Caleb's family to eat. We don't want to tip off Caleb so he knows we're not genuine. His mom's as sweet as shoofly pie, and salty, ginger molasses cookies wouldn't be fair to her."

"I suppose," Sadie's words mumble around a mouth stuffed with cookie. "Does she know her son's a bad apple?"

"Most likely she has no idea she's sheltering a lawbreaker like him."

We pack the washed quilt, the cookies, and a few other essentials Mammi insisted on giving, including a homemade hot mitt. I shake my head. *If this is a homeless person stealing, which I figure it isn't, since Caleb has Dawdi's hat, what would he have for a potholder?* I figure Mammi knows best, despite her moments of getting all mixed up. Dawdi said he'd do the delivery, but we decide this might give us a better chance to look for more clues.

Sadie and I trudge toward the covered bridge trying to decide where to put the basket of goodies, so that any old person doesn't consider it a free gift. Dawdi wants the right thief to get the treats.

"Let's put the basket there." Sadie points to an area beside the covered bridge where the land slopes toward the creek running below the old wooden structure. The wind gusts against the wooden siding of the bridge. It creaks and moans, worn out from stretching from one side of the hill to the other. The creaking of the timber-truss bridge, held together only with wooden pegs, stirs my curiosity about the decrepit passageway. *For one, how old is it? For two, who built it? And for last, why would someone keep stashing stolen stuff here?*

Our knees bend as we navigate down the steep hill toward the grassy bank of the creek. The melted snow left the ground glistening with moisture. The green sprouts of spring growth make a soft, fragile carpet. "This is a good spot, I'd say."

Sadie plops the basket on the ground, then she scans the shadows. "Think the thief's watching us right now?"

I scour the area. Water rushes over rocks in the creek bed. A few chickadees perch in the brush, chirping. Nothing remains of the mysterious pile from the other night.

Sadie and I scan the dark place under the bridge, hunting for clues. Above us, strings of old growth dangle between the tight wooden slats.

Sadie crouches to tuck into a tight space where the bottom of the bridge meets with the sloping earth. Her teal green dress looks pretty against the blackened wood and mossy ground. "If I were homeless, this is where I'd live." Sadie sighs.

"Why, Sadie?"

"If it snows or rains, this is like a roof. I'd catch crawdads in the stream for food and eat the wild onion that grows here.

And that," Sadie huffs as she plods up the bank, "that's an apple tree." She grins like she plans to move in today.

"Well, I see what you mean, but the place still gives me the creeps, on account of the fact that a criminal lives here."

Sadie eyes me. "I thought Caleb was the criminal."

"Oh. Yah. Well, still, he spends an awful lot of time here up to no good."

"True." My cousin nods like a scholar, then hikes to the entryway of the bridge.

We link arms and walk through the covered bridge toward Caleb Miller's home. The most handsome crook in the county.

Too bad. I was gonna marry him. ✳

CHAPTER 12

NO HINT OF GUILT

WE ARRIVE AT CALEB'S house, huffing like two old women. The road to his place stretches long, like a python sunning itself. The Miller's apple trees stand in neat rows. They're just beginning to bud, green dotting the dark brown branches. Sadie bolts toward the thief's house and yells, "Jonah, what are you doing here?"

My tall cousin flashes a smile over his big shoulder from where he stands shooting the breeze with Caleb. "Makin' plans for fishing." My cousin runs his thumbs under his suspenders that mostly hold his olive-colored shirt where it belongs. Jonah stands a good foot taller than Caleb. But then Jonah stands a foot taller than most people. A gentle giant, that's what I call him.

"Fishing with Ca-leb?" Sadie says his name all drawn out in two long, weird syllables. Then she says it again, just in case she wasn't awkward enough the first time. "Fishing with Ca-leb?"

Caleb eyes Sadie, his mouth tips up on one side. "Yes, he is."

He has more nerve than a fox in a house full of super-fat, peckish hens.

"Care to join us?" Caleb palms a walnut, cracks the shell, and pops the meat into his mouth, chewing like he doesn't have a care in the world.

I eye Sadie to send the silent signal of no-way-Jose-we-don't-want-to-fish-with-a-thief. Only Sadie doesn't take hints too well and storms right on. "Well, maybe we will. How would you like that Ca-leb Mil-ler? Hmm?"

Caleb smiles full-faced, then laughs like he and Jonah share a hilarious, inside joke. "I'd like it just fine." He raises an eyebrow at me. "You coming too, Poppy?"

I gag on my spit and take two-million hours to clear my throat before squeaking, "Sure." My face heats to the color of Onkel Abner's late summer plums, I'm sure, partly from lack of oxygen and partly from feeling like a total dummy. I imagine being sucked into sinking sand and swallowed whole. Might be better than this. I step forward. Where did all my plans to snoop around go? "Mammi asked us to drop by with a treat for your family."

Caleb leans in and snatches a cookie from under the tea towel wrapped around the still-warm goodies. "Mmm . . . well, that's kind. What for?" He asks around an enormous bite.

I stare at Caleb to detect any hint of guilt. Any spark of 'gee-I'm-sorry-for-stealing-from-such-nice-folks.'"

But no.

Nothing.

Caleb repeats more slowly, like I'm too slow to grasp his meaning. "Why did she do that, Poppy?"

In my quest for truth, I realize I'm leaning in slightly. Jonah eyes me and runs his thumbs underneath his suspenders more rapidly, bouncing a little like he's nervous. "Yah, how come, Poppy?"

"Oh, um, just because . . . because we thought . . . Mammi thought. Hmm."

Caleb shakes his shaggy blonde head and grins. "Well, why didn't you say so in the first place?" He chuckles like he's such a humorous fellow and my face warms as hot as a sunburn again.

Sadie walks to me, hooks her arm through mine, and lifts her head in the air. "Let's go in and drop off these ginger molasses cookies with Mrs. Miller, Poppy." She tugs on my arm until my feet, that grew roots, unlatch from the ground.

When we're nearly to the front door and just before Sadie knocks in her typical musical way, she yells. "Make sure you wear your fancy new hat, Caleb. For fishing that is." She looks at me and winks a second before Caleb's mom opens the door and invites us inside. ✳

CHAPTER 13

FISHING FOR CLUES

JONAH HOOKS HIS WORM, his tongue protruding from the corner of his mouth. He casts his line into the calm waters of Bontrager's pond. He stands with his usual stance while fishing, one leg back and the whole rest of the top of his body hunched over his rod, as if bracing for an enormous catch to near-drag him into the water. Jonah grins at Caleb who lazes nearby. "Betcha I catch more fish than you, Caleb." My cousin always speaks a little too loud.

Caleb leans back on his elbows, his rod propped on a rock by his feet, the line bobbing and dancing on the mostly calm surface. "I don't doubt that, Jonah, you usually do," he says, slathered in kindness and not even an ounce of sneaky.

Jonah laughs with an open-mouth-so-wide-you-could-catch-flies sort of laugh. "You know I'm right, don't cha, Caleb?" When my sweet-hearted cousin gets excited, he says the person's name he's speaking to at the end of each and every sentence. And fishing ranks at the tippy-top of his favorite things to-do list.

Caleb only replies, "You're always right, Jonah." Caleb knows as well as I do that Jonah probably catches more fish than anyone else.

In his patient, gentle way, Jonah lures in enough brown trout to feed two families almost every time he goes fishing. The lake is more quiet than usual. Maybe Old Man Winter's blast of April snow scared them off. All the bugs know better than to appear so soon in the season. The creatures sense Middlebury's spring weather is as unpredictable as a cat with no tail.

I stand a little ways up the shore from the boys and Sadie. My line tangles in the overgrowth of pondweed for the thousandth time and I reel it in. I train my eyes on Caleb, who sprawls like he has all the time in the world and not a trouble to speak of.

Sadie fidgets beside him and catches my eye. She squints like she wants to telepathically communicate. I shake my head and furrow my brows to let her know I have no clue what squinting eyes mean. I shoot a cut-it-out look and a make-your-self-useful, and an at-least-pretend-to-fish look.

But she only clears her throat and points at Caleb. He stretches out, lies back, and props the big felt hat against his face, most likely to fall asleep and dream up his next crime.

I've had enough of Sadie's cryptic game of charades. "What do you want, Sadie?"

Her mouth gapes like a fish gulping air, then says, "I just wondered if you might be curious about Caleb's hat, same as me." Again, her squinchy eyes and head bobbing attempt to relay a secret message I'm not getting.

Caleb sits up and plops the hat on the top of his head. "What's that, Poppy?"

I look at Caleb, then at Sadie, then at Jonah who frowns at me like I'm acting rude to an honored guest. *Why am I the person everyone is staring at?* I'm not the one who dropped a super-obvious hint about Caleb being a crook.

"What's what?" I say smartly. "I didn't say anything. Sadie did." I point, in case he forgot who Sadie is.

He cocks his head toward Sadie who shakes hers, all wide-eyed and innocent. "I just wondered where you got that hat on your head."

"This?" Caleb points like there are other hats to choose from.

Typical stalling technique.

"Yes, that." Sadie stands, feet apart, hands pressed against her hips, like a billy goat ready to charge. If my heart wasn't thumping so hard inside my rib cage, I'd be tempted to laugh out loud at how puny she looks compared to Jonah and Caleb.

Jonah scratches his head, leaving his hair sticking up like a rooster's comb. "Why you asking that, cousin? What's so special about a hat?" He rocks a little bit, something he does when he gets upset. "Don't you bother Caleb. He didn't do anything wrong."

Caleb notices how the conversation upsets Jonah and stands, dusting dirt from his backside. "I'm okay, Jonah. I don't mind her asking."

He turns his blue-green eyes on me, like he knows I want to know the answer too. "I found the hat by the covered bridge. Right along the bank of the water. Does it belong to you? I asked around, but nobody claimed it."

I shake my head, sure if I move I'll disintegrate into a pile of miniature crumbs, then fly off into the wind. "You found it?" Relief and confusion pick a fight with each other. I swallow the lump in my throat. The terrible disappointment about thinking Caleb was the thief had lodged in my stomach—and now that I know the truth, I'm left feeling tired.

Sadie dives back in. "So you're saying you didn't steal it?" Her eyes still mirror distrust and she continues her incessant squinting.

Caleb snatches the hat from his head. "Why would I steal it?"

"It belongs to my Dawdi, Caleb, that's why," Sadie yells. "He definitely didn't stash his hat by the bridge."

Our handsome schoolmate shakes his head like a ball of string rolls around inside. "You thought . . . ?" Caleb glares at me as his face flushes crimson. His eyebrows lower and he shoves his hands into his pockets, ". . . that I stole from your dawdi?"

Does he feel as badly as I do? I stare at my shoes, the toes covered in dried mud.

He huffs, snatches his fishing rod, and flings the hat at my feet. Sadie swoops in to pluck it up like she's afraid he'll grab it back.

Caleb jerks his head. "I'm sorry, I have to leave."

Always the picture of joy with his smiles and laughter, I've never seen Caleb angry. Again, I swallow the lump stuck in my throat.

I lumber toward him, my shoes feeling as heavy as cement blocks, and say as small and squeaky as a chipmunk with stage fright, "I'm sorry, Caleb." My eyes are dangerously close to spilling tears, but it doesn't matter. "Can you forgive me for thinking you'd steal from my dawdi? We saw you wearing the hat that went missing a few nights ago from Dawdi's barn and . . . "

Standing dead-still, Caleb stares at me like he struggles to figure out my mixed-up brain. He looks at the ground, pokes at a rock with the toe of his shoe, then answers slowly, "I forgive you, Poppy. Always. No use holding grudges."

Jonah breaks in, "Maybe it's the same one who stole all the other stuff from

Mammi and Dawdi. Maybe the same person left it at the bridge."

Sadie leaps on that like a wildcat on a field mouse. "But why, Jonah? I don't understand taking stuff only to leave it in broad daylight. And then not even use it? What's the point? Just plain old meanness?"

Again Jonah rocks, "I saw on the news . . . " At this Jonah gazes at his feet.

No Old Order Mennonite boy should watch television and Jonah knows it. Shame turns him two shades of red lollypop, and then apple magenta, in that order. "I overheard the news talking about a burglar breaking into homes. Stealing things. One time, he hurt the people inside, 'cause they caught him in the act."

Caleb stands by his friend and rests his hand on Jonah's shoulder to calm the rocking motion. "And you suspect the thefts are committed by the same people, Jonah?"

"Could be," Jonah mumbles.

Suddenly the mystery makes me feel like an animal caught in quicksand with no idea how to escape.

Caleb offers, "We'll figure this out together." Still standing with his hand on Jonah's shoulder, he looks at Sadie and me. "All of us. We'll put a stop to it. Somehow." He looks toward the direction of his farm. "But next time, tell me if you have any questions instead of just assuming I'd do something like this. Deal?"

How come he's so much more grown up than the rest of us?

Each of us repeat, "Deal."

All thoughts of fishing fizzle, and the fun sags like a deflated balloon discarded by the shore. We head away from the pond, then split off toward our homes. Questions spin in my mind like a hooked fish twisting on a line. Only I can't reel in the answers or lure them from their hiding places. ✳

CHAPTER 14

EATING HUMBLE PIE — OR COOKIES

NOW BAKING CHOCOLATE CHIP oatmeal friendship cookies for Caleb feels right. He definitely earned a treat for himself. Besides, we need to fortify ourselves. We made a plan to meet during recess at school to discuss how to trap this thief. Jonah graduated last year from student to a hard-working adult, carpentering alongside my onkel at his home-based business, Yoder Furniture. So today it's just Sadie, Caleb and myself. I have no clue which path will lead to answers.

I mix together the memorized ingredients, the recipe an old family favorite. The movement of the whisk through the dry ingredients calms my thoughts spinning off like those blackbirds sporting feathery red patches on their wings and fluttering near the bridge. *Has it really only been a few days since we learned of the mystery? Are we still in over our heads with a real honest-to-goodness burglar in our midst?*

I focus on creaming together the butter and sugar until it looks like whipped frosting, then add vanilla, and finally, the rest of the ingredients: chocolate chips, raisins, and oats. I look around Maam's kitchen, liking the predictability today.

The long wooden table surrounded by eight chairs, calms me, and reminds me of what is most important: God and family. Not mysteries or worries about what might happen or anything else. Being the last kid still in the home, the place is quiet most of the time, probably why Maam doesn't mind me spending so much time helping at Sadie's. She must know I need the companionship, and adventure too, I'll admit.

Maam works in our garden, turning the dirt to prep the ground for planting. I plan to finish the cookies before heading to school. Mornings start early for us, as for most Old Order Mennonites. Hard work is a normal way of life for us. We already ate breakfast at the table, Daad, Maam and I. Cheerful despite the early hour, my parents attend to their work and various chores. I, on the other hand, am as fidgety as a bug in a sock.

I pull the baked batch of cookies from the oven, place them on a rack to cool, then run to snatch my jacket. I package the treats in a brown paper bag and step into the crisp morning air.

I calm myself by reciting the new words I discovered in my crusty old dictionary. Vociferous. *Crying out noisily.* Jouska. *A pretend conversation played out completely inside your head.* And my favorite: Flumadiddle? *Utter nonsense.* Which is what this whole mystery feels like. A big old pile of stinky flumadiddle.

I meet Sadie at the school steps. Words and clues bouncing around like a jar full of marbles tumbling downhill on a bumpy road.

"You look funny," Sadie offers, ever so helpful and blunt.

"Thanks a lot, cousin."

"You know what I mean. You okay?" She asks.

"Not totally. But partly. You know?"

"Yah, I know." Sadie links arms calming my jumbled feelings a little.

"Is Caleb here yet?"

"Yep. Right on time, as usual." Sadie drops her cloak on a hook outside our classroom door. "I can't believe you thought he could be the thief." She casts me a sidelong glance.

I wave the bag of cookies in front of her face. "What?"

I sputter and gulp, trying to force out the words piled in my throat like a log jam. But then I manage, "You know what Sadie? That's a whole lot of flumadiddle. Yah. That's what it is."

Sadie giggles, covering her mouth until her face glows red and tears fill her eyes. "Only joking, Poppy. But that was really funny."

I offer a feeble smile, before starting to laugh myself. "I guess it was." Only now I feel pretty dumb.

"Where'd you get that word? Reading your dictionary again?"

"You know learning new words calms me, Sadie."

"Yah, I know you."

Together we enter the room. I glide into my seat connected to my old-fashioned wooden and iron school desk that sits in front of Caleb. *I feel like a jerk for accusing him of stealing from Dawdi.* I turn and slide the package of cookies onto his oak desktop, not saying a word, hoping he won't tease me.

He smiles and nods, like he recognizes the peace offering for what it is.

I relax a little in my seat as my teacher

talks about birds' nests and how birds use spit to hold their homes all together. Nothing like the bizarre facts of nature to make everything settle back into normal again. *

CHAPTER 15

LAYING THE TRAP

AFTER SCHOOL, SADIE, CALEB and I stroll along the back-country road traveled more by buggies than cars. My thoughts spin like three separate tops on a smooth table.

"What's the plan, Poppy?" Caleb glances at me. "I'd like to catch the person stealing from your dawdi." Rachel buzzed around us the entire time at recess, so we never got the chance to talk about what to do.

Sadie skips ahead until we trail ten feet behind her. She swings around and grins. "I got all the way here in three skips." She jerks her backpack higher on her back, then sets off again, looking like a half-crazed, frilled lizard.

I remember my sixth-grade teacher

holding up a picture of that funny creature, looking almost like it was telling a joke, his mouth wide open. A fan of skin circled his goofy expression and he stood upright, with thin legs to the side, mid-stride. I giggle watching my crazy cousin looking much the same, only she wears a long dress limiting her ability to really go at it.

"Does the thief do anything the same every time? Like coming and taking things at the same time or in the same places?" Caleb's voice pulls me into the present and from my science book lesson from last year.

"Well, he's never taken anything inside the house. Only stuff on the front porch or from the barn," I say.

"That tells me that at least the person's not crazy enough to go inside." Caleb's eyes narrow.

"Well, true." Then I add, sounding a little like I just guzzled an enormous glass of grapefruit juice, "Not yet anyway."

Caleb yells to Sadie, "Hey, Sadie, wait up."

A gust of brisk wind snatches Caleb's hat off his head, spinning it into the sky. For a full five minutes, we dart like birds diving for bread crumbs.

Finally, Caleb leaps and catches his black felt hat in mid-air. He releases a loud victory whoop before tugging his hat down on his head and returning to our spot of collaboration. Caleb's fluffy hair sticks out like straw with no rhyme or reason beneath his hat. "Maybe our thief is the wind."

"Yah." Sadie yells, then stops, rubbing her chin thinking whether the wind thief theory is possible. "Well, probably not," her words thud in a pile.

"Follow me," Caleb says.

We tromp off the road and head through the woods lining the back of Caleb's farm.

After what feels like a gazillion miles, Caleb stops, huffing and puffing. "There." He points to a contraption about a foot tall, with a trigger stick, bent like an old man, and a noose spread in a circle and made of twine.

"What's that?" Sadie rubs her temples, her blonde eyebrows push together in a bunch.

Caleb stoops and grabs a long twig, then taps it on the spot where the loop meets with the ground. The trap springs, grabbing the stick from his hand. The twine bounces in the air. "A snare trap," Caleb says. "Here's my thought. Let's set a trap. Something to help us identify our thief."

"Identify?" Sadie says.

"Yes. Help us figure out who he is," I pipe in, finally finding my voice and my brains.

"But how?" My cousin clamps her arms across her chest. "Can't very well make him fly up in the air by one leg and hang upside down."

"Yah, Caleb, we don't want to actually hurt anyone. Just stop them from hurting Mammi and Dawdi."

"So what kind of a trap could lure the person and catch him red-handed without actually hurting him?"

It's my turn to rub my chin. For some unknown reason that helps me think better. "Pie." I blurt.

"Pie?" Sadie parrots.

"Pie," I repeat.

Caleb grins and winks. "I like how you think, Poppy."

My stomach does a jig.

Sadie huffs, "Would anyone mind filling me in here? I don't have a clue what you two are talking about."

I turn to Sadie, "Pie tempted the crook before. It'll be the perfect bait to bring him again." *

CHAPTER 16

NABBiNG A THiEF

SADIE AND I STOP at Mammi and Dawdi's house on our way home from school, only to find Jonah standing in their living room as if he isn't planning on moving until they see some sense.

We've poked a hornet's nest, for sure. Jonah, who always smiles and whistles, shoots upright like a soldier. A grouchy one. "I don't see how come you won't lock your doors at night, Dawdi." His normally gentle voice bellows as loud as a bullhorn.

Mammi stands beside Jonah, her hand patting his back like he's a baby. She tsk-tsk's him, then says, "The good Lord knows our comings and goings. We can trust him to take care of us." She continues her gentle tap-tap on his wide shoulder blades. "Besides, we've always left our doors open, in case a weary soul or family member needs to come in. This house, these things." She sweeps a hand around the room. "They belong to God. He can pass them on to anyone who might need a little help. That's fine with your Dawdi and me."

"But . . . but . . ." Jonah sputters and huffs air through his mouth discharging all his pent-up frustration. "You could be hurt." With that, he spins on his heel and marches toward the door, stepping around Sadie and me who stand like two wooden poles planted in the entrance.

Mammi only sighs. "Sorry, girls. Jonah's got himself a little worked up is all. Soon, he'll be right as rain."

Is Mammi right about Jonah? I notice how worry rims Jonah's eyes whenever we talk about the thefts. Maybe we should include him in our plan to trap the thief, except he tends to get upset about doing anything that might be seen as wrong. Once when I told him he was my most favorite person in the world he got really red and then said, "You shouldn't say that, Poppy. It's not fair to the others."

Good as gold, Jonah is. No, better keep our plan to solve the mystery to ourselves. Hopefully, we can put his heart at rest regarding Mammi and Dawdi, sooner rather than later.

Sadie snaps me out of my somersaulting thoughts. "Mammi, we'd like to stay over this weekend. All right with you?" This is Sadie's job: to secure the sleepover date so we can start on the trapping part.

Mammi smiles and bobs her head. "Sure, Sadie girl, you know you're always welcome."

We are "in"–the ball officially begins to roll. ✳

CHAPTER 17

A BREAK-IN

SADIE AND I EACH help our maams with chores, so it's almost dinnertime when we head to Mammi and Dawdi's. We stop by Caleb's house to let him know to get everything sorted for the following night when we hope the crook will do his thieving again.

"Hungry, girls?" Mammi stands in the kitchen with her soft cheeks all rosy and an apron drawn around a starched, plum-colored dress. She stirs soup in an iron kettle and looks super chipper. Her pot holds way more than she and Dawdi can manage to eat in a solid week. *Sweet Mammi.*

"What's cooking?" Sadie moves beside Mammi and looks into the pot.

"Wild rice soup." Mammi grabs a handful of shredded cheese, dropping the golden deliciousness into the creamy, hot broth.

"Mmm. My favorite." I lick my lips in anticipation of eating the yummy meal.

Mammie turns to me. "I know, Poppy girl."

My mouth waters when she pours some cream into the mixture, stirring again. "Can I help with anything?"

My Mammi points a bent, arthritic finger to the loaf of bread cooling on a rack. "You can cut that into slices."

Sadie reaches for some bowls in an upper cabinet. "I'll set the table."

Just as if Dawdi senses food is about to be served, he enters the house, his face chapped red from the cool, biting wind. "Smells good in here. And look who I get to eat with. Three beautiful ladies." His eyes squint in a smile. The skin of his eyelids bunch up like loose socks, hanging over his sharp gaze. His bushy eyebrows pull together in the middle like a fuzzy caterpillar.

We all plop into our seats for dinner, Dawdi offering a silent prayer. And, I confess, instead of doing much praying, I spend time reviewing the plan Sadie and Caleb and I made. *Tomorrow night we'll finally have a chance to catch the thief.*

My stomach squirms like a worm in a bait box. I look at my cousin who only slurps her soup and sighs.

A loud noise sounding like glass breaking awakens Sadie and me from our sleep. "Did you hear that?" I whisper to Sadie who snores across the room from me.

She springs up and mumbles several "what's" and "what-are-you-saying's."

"I heard something break, Sadie." My heart hammers like a woodpecker tapping away at the wooden siding of our farmhouse. We aren't expecting Caleb and his trap until tomorrow night.

Besides, the plan did not, in any way—not even a little bit—involve breaking anything.

After taking fifty million years to rouse my cousin and get her out of the bed, we shuffle into the living room where I nail my shin on the low coffee table. I suck in a sharp breath, not wanting to alert the thief to our presence, should he be snooping around.

We inch forward in the dark. Odd shapes and gray shadows envelop the room. All the while my chest thumps like a metal box of shaken marbles, pinging from side to side.

Sadie bumps against my back and we both whisper-yell, "Ow."

I react, "Careful."

We topple like dominoes tumbling against each other in the darkness. I regain my balance with my palms lying flat against the wall. "Listen, Sadie."

"To what?" She hisses.

"Can't you hear that?" I fumble through the front room, then feel my way around the corner, then down, down, down the long breezeway, leading outside. The space serves as a mudroom full of coats and boots, so tripping hazards mark our passage. Long shadows stretch weird on the walls, like phantoms standing watch. I massage my forearms with my hands to rub away the goose bumps from freaking me out more than I already am.

All the while Sadie remains glued to my back like she hopes I might just quit and offer her a piggyback ride. I pull open the door and a spooky, long squeak electrifies all the hairs on my head. If only Mammi and Dawdi didn't just have oil lamps that needed to be lit. Tonight I wish for good, old-fashioned electricity.

Above us, wings flap.

"What in tarnation was that? Do you think that's the thief? If it is, I might just die. I really might, Poppy. I might up and die right here in Mammi and Dawdi's breezeway." Sadie's voice sounds like a jiggly pile of Jell-O, all wobbly.

"Only a screech owl, Sadie. Listen."

"I am listening."

I keep the words inside that really want to come out. Including how a person who talks so much can possibly be listening to anything but her own voice. Or, how speaking too loud might catch you-know-who's attention, something we most definitely do not want to happen. I shake off my shivers.

"I think he's out there." I point into the darkness toward the general direction of the front porch.

"Well, then let's not go that way."

"We are trying to catch him, aren't we?" I whisper back at Sadie.

"No. No, we aren't. We're just little girls."

I turn and face my cousin, eye to eye. "Look, if you want to turn back we can, but this is our chance to get a good look at him."

She fiercely shakes her head "no" in the darkness, her face looking slanted in the gray light of the moon.

I convince myself to peer out the

doorway, only allowing a teeny-tiny bit of my head to show. My face tingles from the crisp night air and I shiver.

Then I see it—the hunched figure of a man. At least I think it's a man. It's hard to tell in the dark. He sprints toward the road, then races in the direction of the covered bridge.

"What's he holding in his arm?"

"I don't know, Sadie, but I have a bad feeling this time."

A cool breeze rushes from the breezeway, pulling my gaze to the six-paned, wood frame window near the entry. "Is that window open or something?" I whisper.

I feel around to locate the big, clunky flashlight my grossdaadi hangs on a hook by the door. Finding it, I switch it on, scanning the room, ending at the window.

"Oh no," I exclaim.

"What?" Sadie sounds like a mouse trapped under a cat. "What is it?"

"The window."

Below the bottom half of the six-paned window, glass glitters on the rough, wooden floorboards. In the middle of the mess sits a rock wrapped in paper. I lean down and pull off the note. Hands trembling, I point the shaky flashlight on the words and read the sloppy, scrawled message aloud. "This is a warning. Beware."

Except the word 'warning' is spelled 'worning.' ✳

CHAPTER 18

A WARNING

THE NEXT MORNING SADIE and I stumble down the stairs to find Dawdi sweeping the broken glass. The old-fashioned corn broom's movement scratches the sparkling heap across the rough, wooden floorboards. Mammi hums as her fried corn meal mush cooks in the iron skillet on the stove. The sweet corn smell drifts through the whole house, mixing with the scent of coffee and warming maple syrup.

I watch Dawdi's back, crisscrossed with gray suspenders, and blink back a ball of tears wanting to explode from my eyes. *Who wants to hurt my Dawdi and Mammi?* They're the most generous and kind people on God's green earth.

Then, quick as a cat doused with water, anger arises in my chest, filling my throat. I'm super-duper, fire-cracker mad.

I clomp from the living room into the kitchen to face Mammi who hums a hymn as she flips a golden corn cake in the iron skillet. A gazillion volcanoes just might erupt and explode out my ears, pouring scalding steam and rude words on everyone near me.

"What do you think now, Mammi? Do you still think this terrible, awful, mean as a snake person deserves cookies and clean quilts?" My voice against the quiet, sizzly popping of the frying mush sounds like nails on a chalkboard. I storm on. "You know what I think? I think the crook deserves to be caught and tied up and dragged with rope to jail to rot and feel bad for the rest of his life." My speech putters out, the volcano running out of lava. Instantly, shame smolders in my chest, neck and face about yelling at Mammi. I wish I could crawl under the carpet with the spiders and disappear until everyone forgets my rude anger.

Dawdi walks his slow and steady way toward me, shuffle, shuffle, shuffle, then rests his warm hand on my shoulder. His voice is so gentle it nearly hums a low, soothing song. "It's easy to see why you're mad, Poppy. I admit, I can't get my brain to understand the purpose in all this. But God is the judge, not us."

Tears once again threaten to spill from my eyes—swimming as if I wasn't a girl, but a fish under water. The burning tightness in my chest eases when I lean against Dawdi's clean, cotton shirt and sob. His clothes smell like sunshine, dried outdoors on Mammi's stretch-across-the pasture clothesline. *I feel like a two-year-old instead of a twelve-year-old, but I don't mind.* Dawdi pats my back, hushing my cries and calms my racing heart.

At that moment, Jonah steps into the mud room and looks around, first at the pile of glass and the broken window, then at Dawdi. He clenches his fists at his sides, glances at his feet, then glares at us. "I told you this would happen. I told you so you'd be smart and lock your doors. But you didn't listen and now look at this." He nearly yells, "Won't you listen to me now?"

He's nearly as angry as I was less than a minute ago, like a hornets' nest destroyed by a baseball bat. Then Jonah stands stock still as the morning after a heavy snow, his eyes brimming with tears. "What happened to your hand, Dawdi?" Jonah's words soften and flow so teeny tiny, despite his big, grown-man body.

"Nothing to worry over, Jonah. Just a little cut is all."

I didn't notice the gauze wrapped around Dawdi's thumb. Jonah's voice climbs a notch and he whines, "What happened, Dawdi?" My cousin's eyes look like a jack rabbit backed into a corner.

"Cut it on some glass, but I'm fine. Not to worry."

Jonah shakes his head, rubs his eyes, and bawls like a baby.

Dawdi removes his hand from my shoulder and walks to Jonah and embraces him. He whispers in Jonah's ear, something I can't make out. Afterward Jonah only nods and leaves the room, tears in his eyes still, swiping them away with the back of his big, rough hand. The whole world flips upside down, shaken like a snow globe.

Dawdi only stares after my tall, strong cousin lumbering away, looking more like a little boy than a man today. Jonah's head and shoulders droop, as if he lugs a heavy sack of feed across his neck and broad shoulders.

"Where's Jonah going?" Sadie shifts from foot to foot, impatient with all the drama of the morning. She eyes breakfast lying like a feast on the kitchen table, complete with cinnamon-honey butter, maple syrup, and a mountain of fried corn meal mush rectangles.

Dawdi waves his hand toward the kitchen, then shuffles toward the table. "He's bringing some tools to fix the window. I have an old window in the barn about the size of the broken one. Jonah knows where they are and is handy about those things. Said he wants to fix the window all on his own. Work helps the heart in a way worrying never does."

Through the windows, we all watch Jonah plod toward the barn, slow as a turtle with a broken leg, stopping by the wood chopping block for his toolbox. He stands there for a time, looking as dejected as I've ever seen him.

Thoughts press into my mind. He's always prepared, my cousin. *Slow in some ways, but smart as a whip in others, and handy as they come. And sweeter than maple syrup after the last freeze.*

In the past, I observed my cousin heft cinder blocks as if they were cotton balls. I also watched him retrieve a frightened kitten stuck in a tree, carrying the tiny feline as gentle as could be in his rough, large hands. Jonah is as loyal and sweet as they come.

He lifts his toolbox, looking tired, then glances back at the house. Yep, he's prepared for anything, even a broken window. And willing to do anything to take care of Mammi and Dawdi. ✳

CHAPTER 19

HONEYED AND FEATHERED

THE CLOUDS SPREAD LIKE cotton balls stretched thin and long by a child's hand across the moon, across the sky. The trees bounce against the black, star-dotted night. The hush and whoosh of the evening breeze calms my jumpy-as-a-grasshopper nerves. My plan must work *tonight*, or else Caleb, Sadie and I will never find the crook who's done so much damage.

"I'm going to head to bed, girls." Dawdi stands from his chair, his bones popping as he stretches. "I'm as rusty as an old hinge." My dawdi chuckles at his joke, then does something I never once witnessed him doing. He ambles to the front door and locks it with a click.

He's scared too. The thought sours my stomach, but at least I won't worry as much after Sadie and I leave for home tomorrow—that's if our plan works.

Dawdi offers a hand to Mammi who blinks awake from her snoring, sitting-up sleep. "Ready for bed, Maam?" Dawdi often calls my Mammi "mom" and I like the way he still cares about her, so sweet and careful.

She bobs her head and her hips see-saw from side to side, inching her rear to the edge of the over-stuffed chair. "I wasn't sleeping, you know." Her eyelids flutter against the dim light of the gas lamps hanging on the walls like torches. "Just resting my eyes."

"Yes, I know." Dawdi's grin spreads from ear to ear drawing his eyes into a squint. "You never are, dear."

"Oh you." Mammi swats his arm, then links hers with his. "Always the teaser."

"Are Aendi and Onkel still getting home tomorrow?" Sadie inquires.

"Right after lunch, they said. Hired a driver to bring them home from their visit with Esther. She had her baby girl, you know. Named her Lily-Anne after my dear Maam, long gone now. God rest her soul," Mammi says.

I did know. Mammi was thrilled about the arrival of her fifth, great-grand baby and about her being my great-great-grandmother's namesake too. Every time the ladies get together for a quilting frolic, Mammi settles in the corner in the comfy rocker, crocheting lines of pink flowers for an afghan as if she painted them.

Once I caught her snoring and, honest-to-goodness, her fingers kept moving, crocheting a rose-shaped stitch. After a time, she awoke with a soft snort and looked at her hands, then picked right up where she'd left off, literally crocheting in her dreams. Maybe Mammi really never fell asleep, as she claimed. Maybe she was just resting her eyes.

Dawdi places a hand on my head. "Us two old fogeys sure loved having you girls here. Don't be strangers just 'cause your Aendi and Onkel will be home."

"We won't, Dawdi," I promise.

After Mammi and Dawdi leave the room, Sadie and I face each other. "I'm not sure about our plan," Sadie whispers. "I just don't know now, especially since whoever-it-is broke a window."

"Caleb doesn't know about that and will be here soon with the trap." I pause, rolling the whole situation over and over in my head like a tumbling tumbleweed from the wild west. I read about tumbleweeds once in a mystery book. In it, a hat stuck to the pin-prickly spines of the golden-brown plant in its travels, scaring the main character silly, who thought the tumbling thistle was the villain chasing him faster than humanly possible.

"I'll set out the pie. Hopefully Caleb brings the honey and feathers," Sadie says.

"Hopefully the thief falls for our trap. Hopefully this will be it." I've had enough of mysteries, broken windows, and dark figures darting into the night.

I shuffle into the kitchen and nab the apple pie from its spot, cooling on the windowsill. A brisk breeze whistles through the cracked-open window. I peer into the dark yard between the barn and chicken coop and pasture. I spot Caleb sauntering into the yard as if it's perfectly normal to visit at 9:00 at night carrying an enormous jar of honey and a bag stuffed with chicken feathers. Sadie and I move toward the front door to meet him.

"Got everything?" Sadie whispers, stepping onto the front porch.

"Yep." Caleb lifts the golden jar from his very own honeybees, a big contribution to the hunting-of-crooks business. "And I brought some feathers." He grins in the moonlight. "Maam killed a hen for dinner tonight."

Sadie gasps. "Why'd you have to go and tell us that?" She shudders and rubs her hands up and down her arms to smooth the hair and goose bumps. "Makes this even more creepy." She leans toward Caleb. "He broke Dawdi's window, you know? Put a rock right through it."

Caleb jerks back and hollers, "Are you serious?" A wrinkle deepens between his bunched brows, like a fresh furrow in a plowed cornfield.

"Shhh," I say.

"That's terrible," Caleb says, still too loud. Then a look sweeps across his face, reminding me of Michael the archangel, ready for battle. "Well, it ends tonight."

Sadie bounces on her toes, a bundle of nervous energy.

I balance the pie on the porch railing. Caleb gets to work on the trap, rigging the pie pan to an invisible fishing line, trailing up and over the rafter that props up two hinged buckets one filled with amber honey and the other loaded with feathers. If the thief takes the bait and grabs the pie, honey and feathers will douse the culprit, catching him right there on the spot, or at least making him easy to identify later. Honey and feathers are not a simple mixture to clear away.

"Now what?" I ask, wondering about our role for the rest of the evening.

Caleb moves a rocking chair into the shadowy overhang of the porch railing, just out of sight. "Now we wait. Or, at least, I wait. No need for two girls to stay outside in the dark and the cold all night. Too dangerous."

Shivers tickle cold on my neck as I think about how easily Caleb disappeared, no longer visible or easy to identify—any ol' person could hide without even trying hard.

"Thanks, Caleb, for your help. It's sure nice of you," I say.

"Happy to help. Besides, your Mammi and Dawdi don't deserve to be treated this way and I want it to stop."

"Will you be okay out here until you-know-who arrives?" Sadie asks.

"Yep. Used to it. Daad and I hunt often enough. We stay still in the cold for hours on end."

"All right. Well, if you're sure," My cousin murmurs looking less-than-sure herself.

Sadie and I pad inside, closing the front door, this time leaving it unlocked in case Caleb needs to escape an attacker. We go to the front parlor with the windows overlooking the porch, turn off the gas valves of the lamps, and wait. Our elbows perch atop the back of the sofa, heads cradled in our palms, fingers fanning across our cheeks. Our eyes fixate on the porch and the darkness and beyond. ✳

CHAPTER 20

To Catch a Thief

A COMMOTION WAKES US. My cousin and I leap to our feet, and peer out the window at a scene almost funny, if my insides didn't jump around so much. A grown man yells and swats at hundreds of feathers floating in the sky, the white of each plume catching the silvery light of the moon.

"Get off. What is this? Help, I'm being attacked." Whoever it is flails his arms and legs like a jumping jack with dozens of chiggers in his pants.

"Come on." Sadie and I rush to the front entry. I fling open the door to watch the wild jerks of our crook, now so close we can net him.

"Now," I yell. "He won't get away this time."

Sadie and I pounce, dropping Dawdi's enormous catfish net over the man's dark, crazy jumping and twisting. Caleb appears from the darkness brandishing a bat, which I know he'd never use unless we were in mortal danger.

"Ow. What're you doin'? What's this all about?" A voice inside the net bellows.

Sadie leaps on his back, like a bull rider determined to hold onto a leaping, twisting beast, even if he tries to bolt toward the covered bridge.

I pause. *I know that voice.* Know that distinct, slow way of talking. Caleb drops the bat to his side. *He knows too.*

"Jonah?" My mouth hangs open wide enough to catch a mason jar-sized swarm of flies.

The man in the net turns to me. "Poppy, what on earth are you doin' with all this?" The moonlight casts strange shadows across my cousin's face.

"What are you doing, Jonah Zook?" Sadie yells in his ear from her piggy-back position.

Jonah's movements stop, like all the fight jolts out of him. He hangs his head, slumps his shoulders while Sadie sticks to his back like Amish wood glue. "You'll think I'm a traitor. I know you will. And maybe yer right, but I did it 'cuz I had to. I just did. You gotta believe me."

Up until his confession, I thought he must have just been in the wrong place at the wrong time. Panic and tears penetrate Jonah's voice. I steady him with my hand. "Let's all calm down and go sit on the porch and talk."

Sadie clings to Jonah's back as he lumbers toward the porch clutching a huge bag in one hand and a net over his head and upper torso. She must figure she might as well hitch a free ride out of it. Besides, her fleshy, shoeless feet hang off his sides and I shiver thinking about her bare toes in the cold, frosted grass.

Sadie slides down Jonah's back. After

freeing him from the catfish net, we sit on the steps and pick feathers one-by-one off his head and shoulders.

"Jonah, tell me you aren't the one. Tell me you didn't steal all of those things from Mammi and Dawdi." My words sound softer than they feel in my brain. I want to yell. I want to shake my kind-hearted-never-hurt-a-flea cousin. I want to dump more honey and feathers on him, and then do it all over again.

Jonah sits as still as a stone statue. If it weren't for his eyes, wide as an owl's surrounded by white feathers, and the silvery stream of tears falling down his cheeks, plus the guilty look on his face, I'd question if I were right.

"How could you?" I whisper trying not to cry myself.

The commotion must have startled Dawdi from his dreams and snores. He steps onto the porch and quietly stands behind Jonah, placing one hand on Jonah's head despite the sticky mess.

"Sometimes," Dawdi says, somehow understanding the whole situation from just one glance. "Sometimes we get an idea in our head that, try as we might, just won't shake loose. That's what happened with Jonah." Dawdi sighs. "And I blame myself. Jonah shared his concern for our safety. He asked us to lock our doors. Only I figured there was no use. We never locked them before and were just fine. But I can be stubborn and . . . "

Jonah stands and whirls around to face Dawdi. "No, Dawdi. You're the nicest person ever and were only trusting in Jesus and His per-tection. I messed everything up, 'cuz I worried you'd get hurt like them people on the TV at The Pantry. They got robbed and when they heard a noise and came out to see what was the matter, they were hurt, that's what happened, Dawdi. They were hurt. And I jus' couldn't allow it. I needed you to see and maybe get just a little bit scared, so you'd be careful." My strong cousin chokes on a sob. "I didn't want to steal all them things, but I was so afraid you'd be hurt too and I couldn't let that happen. I just couldn't let them hurt you, same as they hurt them other folks."

Dawdi hushes Jonah softly, then pulls him in for a bear hug, though sticky honey and feathers coat my cousin. "It's okay. It's okay," Dawdi repeats over and over again.

Sadie, ever honest and blunt blurts, "It was you all along? So . . . what you're saying is that you stole from Dawdi and Mammi to teach them to lock their doors?" Her expression looks like she's trying to put together pieces from one puzzle with another, and finds out they don't fit.

"Yes," I speak up. "Jonah thought if he took enough things, Dawdi would start locking his doors."

Caleb finally asks, "Jonah, did you break that window then?" He says it like he feels sorry for Jonah, not angry, like Caleb understands getting mixed up and making the wrong choices.

Jonah slumps onto the porch swing like an enormous sack of potatoes, like he can't hold himself up any longer. "I'm so sorry. I'm so sorry." He rocks back and forth a little. "I planned to fix it the next day, just like I planned to bring all them things home to Dawdi and Mammi. They just wouldn't listen." Jonah looks at Dawdi, his round eyes wide and sad, his cheeks chapped and red. "I'm really sad about your hand. I wouldn't ever hurt you on purpose. Not ever."

"Only a little scratch. Not to worry. All's well that ends well." Dawdi's rumbly voice slows my heart from a thousand miles an hour to a hundred. I suck in a deep breath to calm myself more. Dawdi speaks again, slow and careful. "Jonah, look at me." He waits until Jonah looks in his eyes. "All is forgiven."

"Really, Dawdi? Can you really forgive me?" Jonah's voice sounds like begging, like a hungry dog looking at a hand full of bones, but isn't sure if it's okay to take one.

"Always, Jonah."

"Umm," Sadie interrupts the sweet moment. "I've never told anyone this before, but I'm gonna tell you now." She steps toward Jonah and stands up tall then clears her throat as if jammed with toast. "I only pretend to be brave and tough." She looks at her bare feet. "I used to go into Maam and Daad's room every night and place my finger under their noses, one by one, just to make sure they hadn't kicked the bucket. You know, stopped breathing and all. But then Maam told me something that helped. She said every single breath is from God and He knows the best time for that to end. I don't need to worry that He'll get that wrong. He's God after all." Sadie, suddenly as wise as a holy man of God, minus the long scraggly beard, grins at Jonah and Jonah grins up at her from his place on the wooden swing.

Then she plucks a feather from Jonah's sticky cheek, and blows it off her pointer finger, "Well, that's enough of that. Now, how's he gonna get de-chicken-ified?"

We notice the feather floating from side to side in the shape of a smile. I giggle seeing my big cousin looking so funny and forlorn, like an enormous owl waiting to go to jail.

Once I start laughing, the rest of group joins in, even Jonah who's laugh wavers between silent shaking-shoulder laughs to full-on honks.

The week that started out so full of creepy questions, ended with love, laughter, and forgiveness. I snap a picture in my mind, since we Old Order Mennonites don't take photos, and I hold the image in my brain, not wanting to ever, ever, ever forget Jonah's open-mouth smile and Dawdi's scrunchy-wrinkled grin. Yep, these are my people. Not perfect, but so full of love, a tall boy with a heart as giant as an elephant's might even steal a person's hat to prove it.

The moon smiles, suspended high in the black sheet of a sky. The trees applaud and laugh with us. *Yes, all's well that ends well, just as Dawdi said.* ✳

Acknowledgements

Writing the Middlebury Mystery series was a heart kind of work. Connecting with and capturing some of my heritage–the Mennonite and Amish way of life and the old, family recipes–made me happy.

First, I'd like to thank my family, my mom and dad, for raising me to know and love Jesus. And to my family members who are with the Lord–thank you for your faithfulness and your heart to live well and love well. Thank you for showing your commitment through the works of your hands and in the food you shared. I especially treasure the old, crusty recipe cards passed on from my Grandma Yoder.

Thank you to my girls Abby, Emma, and Hannah, to my sister, Christy, and to my amazing writer's group including my dear friends Diane, Aimee, Carlye, and my friend Laura, who listened to, read, and offered feedback on these stories. Your wisdom, suggestions and ideas were so helpful and appreciated.

Thank you Debbie Allen for your amazing editing and to Scoti Domeij, who spent countless hours on these books, editing and adding your artistic layout and cover design.

Thank you to my husband, Michael, who offers me his support in marketing and promoting my books, and who constantly encourages me and cheers me on to pursue this writing that fills me with such joy—I love you and I like you.

And finally, thank you to Jesus, who is ever faithful and loving without bounds. I dedicate this and every other work I write to You.

About Holly

Growing up traveling the world as a m i l i tary brat, Holly developed a love for different places and people. From the ancient ruins of a Turkish castle-in-the-sea to waving fields of Indiana corn, her experiences inspire her stories. Her Midwestern Amish and Mennonite family tree from her salt-of-the-earth heritage color her point of view.

Holly married a Colorado man and together they enjoy adventures with their five kids. To encourage each child to thrive in their individual gifts, Holly home schooled their children.

Holly wrote for Good Catch Publishing for five years and won their 2018 Writer of the Year award. She also wrote for Cook Communications.

Holly draws joy from igniting a love for storytelling in her students. For more than 12 years, she's taught creative writing classes at home-school co-ops. Holly also served as an online school teacher and now teaches creative writing for a Homeschool Academic Program in a Colorado Springs public school district, where she utilizes out-of-the-box avenues to inspire imaginative writing.

In Holly's free time, you'll find her watching cooking shows or writing at a local coffee shop with a white mocha and a smile. ✻

Connect with Holly:
Facebook:

https://www.facebook.com/
AuthorHollyYoderDeherrera/

Blog/Website:

https://hollyyoderdeherrera.wordpress.com

Closed Facebook Book Club

Middlebury Mystery Series Book Club

Middlebury Mystery Book Club Questions

Talk about this book with your parents, grandparents, siblings, or teacher. It's even more fun to read the same book with three or four of your friends.

Ask your parents if you can start a book club. Talk about the best time and place to meet, and how often your book club will get together. After you talk about this book, your book club might even complete a 3-D reading activity.

Below are some questions to jumpstart your discussion with your parents, siblings, or friends.

1. If you could trade places with any character in the book, just for fun who would you choose, and why?

2. Poppy's cousin Jonah has an intellectual disability, which can include limitations in communication, learning, problem-solving, reasoning, and social and self-care skills. An intellectual disability is not a disease or a mental illness.

Most individuals with an intellectual disability can learn to accomplish many things. However, learning requires more time and effort.

Sometimes, just because a person with a disability isn't as skilled at some things, doesn't mean they aren't gifted in other ways. For example, Jonah is physically strong, kind, loyal, and protective of those he loves.

Do you know anyone who's disabled? If so, what talents have you noticed in that person?

3. If you could add one more chapter, what would you write, and why?

4. Do you think there is ever an excuse to do something bad to help someone or

make something good happen, like Jonah did? Explain your thoughts.

5. Talk about one thing you learned from this story—a warning, a way to help others, or a lesson about right and wrong.

3-D Reading Activities

Three-D reading means reading, then diving in, and creating something yourself. Try some of the book-themed activities below.

1. Word Picture Painting

Answer the questions below to create a word painting. Choose a place in your imagination where you want to play or think about a mystery to solve. Make believe you're there.

Now, jot down words for each of the five senses.

- What do you see?
- What do you hear?
- What do you feel on your skin?
- What do you smell?
- What do you taste?

Read the answers all together. Great job. You just painted a picture with words.

2. Kill 'Em with Kindness Ginger Molasses Cookies

Bake up a batch of "Kill' Em with Kindness Ginger Molasses Cookies," then give them to someone who could use some kindness—the non-killing kind.

Ingredients:
8 teaspoons butter
1 cup brown sugar
1 egg
1/3 cup molasses
1 teaspoon baking soda
2 cups flour
1 teaspoon ginger

1 teaspoon cinnamon
½ teaspoon ground cloves
½ teaspoon salt
½ cup white sugar

Directions:
Cream the butter, brown sugar, and molasses, and then add the egg. Mix until combined.

Sift together the baking soda, flour, ginger, cinnamon, ground cloves, and salt. Combined the dry ingredients and the wet ingredients together until just mixed.

Chill for an hour or more in the refrigerator. Scoop out into walnut-sized balls and roll in white sugar. Bake on a greased cookie sheet at 350 degrees for 8-10 minutes.

3. "Heal Even a Broken Leg" Chicken Noodle Soup with Homemade Broth

Know anyone who's sick? Why not make them a batch of "Heals Even a Broken Leg" Chicken Noodle Soup? Even if it doesn't make them all better, they'll most definitely feel loved.

Homemade Chicken 'Bone' Broth
Prep time: 10 minutes
Total time: 5-24 hours

Ingredients:
4-5 pound whole chicken, or bones of a pre-roasted rotisserie chicken. Save meat for soup.
2 medium yellow onions, quartered
3 carrots, scrubbed or peeled and cut in half
3 celery ribs with leaves, cut in half
5-6 garlic cloves unpeeled, cut in half
1 large bay leaf
3-5 sprigs fresh thyme
5 sprigs fresh, flat-leaf parsley
2 teaspoons kosher or sea salt
1/2 teaspoon whole black peppercorns (not ground)
1 tablespoon apple cider vinegar
Enough water to fill the pot

Directions:

Place the chicken or rotisserie chicken bones in a 6-quart stockpot. Add the rest of the ingredients and cover with water to within an inch below the top of the pot. Place a lid on the pot, bring to a boil, then reduce to a simmer. Keep the pot covered while simmering. If the liquid reduces too much, add more water.

If you use the whole raw chicken, after two hours, remove the chicken from the pot, and let it cool. Remove as much meat as possible, then place all the bones and skin back in the pot and simmer the stock 4-24 hours. The longer the stock simmers, the more flavorful and nutritious.

Strain the stock through a fine mesh colander or cheesecloth into a large bowl. Discard the bones, vegetables, and herbs.

"Heal Even a Broken Leg" Chicken Noodle Soup

Ingredients:
3 tablespoons butter

1 cup carrots, diced
¾ cup celery, diced
1 medium onion, diced
meat from chicken
3 quarts chicken broth (homemade is best)
Meat from chicken
1/2 pound egg noodles
Fresh, flat-leaf parsley, chopped

Directions:
Melt the butter over medium heat in a large stock pot and add onion, carrots, and celery and cook until slightly softened. Then add chicken stock and bring to a boil. Add the diced chicken. Before serving, add the egg noodles and cook until soft. Top with fresh parsley.

4. Perspective in Art.
Try drawing a road or even railroad tracks using perspective. What is perspective? It means that things that are far away look smaller and things that are closer look larger. So, if you're standing in the middle of a straight road, the part closest to you

will look wider and it will get thinner and thinner the further it goes away from you.

First, on a blank piece of paper, draw a horizontal line close to the top of the page. Next, draw a dot someplace on the horizontal line. Use a ruler to draw the sides of the road. Place the end of the ruler on the dot and angle the ruler so it creates a wider road line at the bottom of the page. You will do this for each side of the road.

If you want to draw a road, draw lines down the middle of the road. Or if you prefer railroad tracks, draw the railroad ties. Just remember that the further away the railroad ties or road lines are from you, the smaller they appear. Have fun adding details, like trees and flowers. Add a mountain range to make the close-up items appear larger.

5. Caleb's Beautiful Honey Bees
Find out all you can about bees and honey. Check out a book from the library about how bees make honey and draw a picture that shows the whole process from start to

finish. Next time you see a bee, instead of screaming and running away, why not stand very still and observe the bee. And, maybe, just maybe, say a super soft, "Thank you."

6. Jump Rope Like Sadie and Rachel
Jumping rope is a great way to exercise and to build coordination. Buy a jump rope and start tracking your progress over the course of several weeks. Each day, mark down how many continuous jumps you do without stopping.

Graph your results to see if you gained or lost jumps. Maybe even observe whether there's a connection between how well you do and how much sleep you got, how healthy you ate that day, or how much exercise you got prior to jumping rope.

7. Conquer Your Fears
Sometimes fear influences us to do things that aren't the best for us, or for those around us, like Jonah stealing things to convince Dawdi and Mammi to lock their doors.

Are you afraid of anything? Share your feelings with your parents, then talk about positive ways to deal with your fear.

Here are some ideas I came up with for my daughter who was afraid of robbers breaking into her room:

- Pray.
- Make sure the windows are locked.
- Turn on a song that makes you feel happy and calm inside.
- When feeling panicky, take in a deep breath for four seconds and slowly breathe out for five seconds.
- Next, look around the room and name *five* things that you love, like a favorite stuffed animal, a toy, or blanket.
- Then name *four* things that are your favorite color.
- Name *three* that are soft and squooshy.
- Name *two* that begin with the letter B.
- And finally, name *one* person that loves you who would do anything to keep you safe.

- Memorize Bible verses that fit your fear. When you feel afraid, pray the Bible verse as a prayer.

Here are a few good ones for you to look up in your Bible:

- Isaiah 41:10
- Jeremiah 29: 11-13
- Philippians 4:13
- Romans 8:38 (This is my personal favorite.)

Remember you are never alone. God sees you and loves you.

Other Books by Holly

The Middlebury Mystery Series for Ages 7-9

The Middlebury Mystery series includes:

- Middlebury Mystery Book Club Questions: Talk about each book, or even more fun: Start a book club and read the Middlebury Mystery series with three or four of your friends.

- A closed Facebook group, Middlebury Mystery Book Club, to provide homeschoolers, teachers, tutors, and grandparents with ideas to inspire great conversations about this mystery series and to explore important life-application principles.

- 3-D Reading Activities for Homeschoolers and Creative Parents
- Old-Timey Mennonite recipes in *The Root Cellar Mystery*

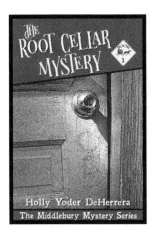

Book 1: The Root Cellar Mystery

Old Order Mennonite cousins, Poppy and Sadie, suspect "A re-e-a-a-al criminal" is staying at Aendi Hannah's bed and breakfast. Then a missing dog, a mysterious code, creepy creaks, and a floating light in the dark of night only make Poppy and Sadie more jumpy and suspicious of their strange, elderly guest. Even trusting Aendi Hannah wants to keep an eye on her snowy headed guest.

After spotting wads of green bills in Ms. Lindy's large trunk, the sleuthing cousins wonder: *Was Ms. Lindy just released from prison and is she a thief?* To figure out what this little old, Mennonite grandmother is up to, the junior detectives spy on their mysterious guest. Why has Ms. Lindy come to Middlebury, Indiana, and what is the puzzling stranger searching for in Aendi Hannah's root cellar?

Confused by Ms. Lindy's odd behavior and an accidental discovery in an old-timey recipe journal, the nosy amateur sleuths hit a dead end. Will Poppy and Sadie's snoopery solve the mystery surrounding Ms. Lindy's past in this cozy mystery in the children's Middlebury Mystery series? ✳

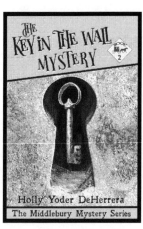

Book 2: The Key in the Wall Mystery

A bad back laid up energetic Aendi Hannah, who's likely going stir crazy. Poppy and Sadie fix up the rooms for guests staying at the Aendi Hannah's bed and breakfast in Middlebury, Indiana. While cleaning, Poppy and Sadie discover a key behind a broken baseboard in the guesthouse. *Who hid the key that looks like a skeleton's bony finger, and why?*

Their crazy quilt clues—an old cast iron key, 70-year-old letters promising a great treasure, a lost, buried time capsule, and a hidden, secret room—lay out no real pattern or direction. The trail grows cold, like the back burner on Aendi Hannah's big, old gas stove.

Twelve-year-old, amateur sleuth Poppy worries: Will their snoopery discover any new leads to follow? And how will the Old Order Mennonite, junior detectives find time to solve this mystery while attending school, cooking meals, and taking care of a household, plus guests?

Are the mystifying lock and treasure lost forever? Or are Poppy and Sadie on a wild goose chase in this cozy mystery in the children's Middlebury Mystery series? ✳

Book 3: The Covered Bridge Mystery

What kind of creep lurks just waiting to steal from Mammi or Dawdi? Poppy and Sadie never expected a real, honest-to-goodness burglar to strike in their close-knit, Old Order Mennonite community in Middlebury, Indiana. The pie-swiping culprit mystifies everyone by stashing all the stolen evidence inside the dusky-dark, covered bridge near Dawdi's farm.

Is the thief-on-the-loose tempting the suspicious cousins to catch him—or her? Jonah, who's developmentally disabled and distraught, fears the burglar will hurt his grandparents. And to make matters worse, Mammi and Dawdi refuse to lock their barn and house—even at night. Using an apple pie as bait, the junior detectives set a trap. Will these amateur sleuths nab the criminal or will the bandit remain on the run in this cozy mystery in the children's Middlebury Mystery series? ✳

For Middle School and High Schoolers

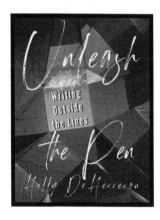

Unleash the Pen. Writing Outside the Lines: *Where has the joy and love of writing for tweens and teens gone?* Too often Holly DeHerrera hears kids say, "I hate writing," or parents say, "I'm so frustrated. I have to force my child to write."

Discover the power of language and the joy of writing. Writing involves far more than mastering the mechanics. Like that old saying, "Putting the cart before the horse," if a student doesn't love writing, or entertain at least a joyful tolerance, stressing rules without free expression chokes imaginative creativity and critical thinking skills.

A student's ability to write affects student achievement in all subject areas. *Unleash the Pen. Writing Outside the Lines* ignites a love for writing and self-expression through words. DeHerrera's positive vision of writing lays out an alternative plan to teach writing that combines writing instruction with diverse, creative writing projects.

Students dive into a topic of their choosing, while experimenting with a variety of fun writing assignments with authentic connections to their lives and their studies. Each self-guided, creative writing incentive leads the student to learn by writing.

Unleash the Pen. Writing Outside the Lines is designed for students to independently work at their own pace, or over the course of a 36-week school year. This teacher-friendly, multi-genre curriculum motivates your students to leap into the adventure of writing. Available Winter 2020. ✳

Young Adult Fiction

The Orphan Maker's Sin: Ella is drawn back to Turkey to solve the mystery of who killed her father—a colonel in the Air Force—and why.

When she meets Murat, a handsome

Turkish man, her dreams for a new beginning soar. Exposed family secrets and betrayal tear Murat and Ella apart, tormenting Murat and testing Ella's faith in everyone who loves her. Will the struggle threatening Ella's truth close her heart to receive or give love—or forgiveness? *

THE COVERED BRIDGE MYSTERY

THE COVERED BRIDGE MYSTERY

Made in the USA
Columbia, SC
22 March 2021